SEXY IN STILETTOS

NANA MALONE

For Manteh "Mantesco 'That's me." Darfoor" You will be missed. Thank you for teaching me to speak my mind.

Erik and Siaki, I love you always. Thank you for loving my lists.

Misty, the words, "Thank You" will never be enough.

Marcie, this will be our year, I promise you.

Megs, Ten, Naad & Cyn, thank you for keeping me sane.

PROLOGUE

HE LOOKS READY TO KILL ME.

Jaya Trudeaux searched her father's usually impassive, though now clearly angry, features. Furrowed brows, check. Tight lips, check. Throbbing vein above his left brow accompanied by a slight twitch in the left eye, courtesy of a long ago tango with a door jamb, check and check. Yep, Pierre was pissed.

Jaya dragged her eyes from her father's glare and focused on the All-Tech Conference selection committee, giving them her best, sweet-girl-next-door meets competent-business woman, meets fellow-nerd smile. This she knew how to do. She understood the client's needs, what it would take to pull off a conference of their magnitude, and that these guys were more SyFy channel than MTV. They wouldn't be swayed with a flashy marketing presentation. They wanted someone who understood their world. Too bad it wasn't the presentation her father wanted her to give.

As Jaya closed, she looked each of the selection committee

members in the eye to make the connection. "Trudeaux Events might not have the flash of Starbuck like some of our competitors—" she indicated the placard with their list of competition. They'd all made pitches and most had gone the more flash than substance route. *Suckers.* "But we understand your needs. And we can meet them."

Her fellow nerds beamed at her. Maybe it was the Battlestar Galactica reference. Maybe they recognized a kindred soul. Maybe they liked her legs. Either way, Trudeaux Events would certainly make the top two candidates for the conference. As the conference would bring well over twenty thousand attendees to San Diego, it would be a huge boon for the event company to land the business. If they were selected, maybe her father would finally make her an event lead.

As soon as the last handshakes were dealt and Brett James, the president of All-Tech thanked them for their time, Pierre Trudeaux indicated the door. Jaya's stomach dropped. *Well damn.* Worst thing was, he had Derrick Cooley, Trudeaux's VP of Corporate Events, trailing right behind him as they exited the boardroom. This couldn't be good.

They were probably pissed she hadn't gone through with their approved presentation. Derrick had pushed for something flashier, wanting to capture the client's attention, and had refused to listen to her ideas for the presentation. Not to mention he hated her. How the hell she'd ever thought she wanted to marry that asshole was beyond her. She must have been high.

Back stiff, she exited out the closest door and started her explanations before they could get a word in edgewise. "I know that's not the original presentation you talked about, but I'm uniquely attuned to this market and I feel like—" She didn't finish. Both of them shot her looks so cold she could feel the icicles forming in her gut.

"In my office, Jaya," her father said.

This. Was. Not. Good. Okay. Plan B time. She wasn't above begging. Jaya wanted this client. *Needed* this client. She'd gone out and recruited this business. It was hers. If they gave the account to Derrick, or worse, to her sister, Tamara, she'd have a fit.

Once in Pierre's austere office, Jaya settled in one of the guest chairs she knew her father selected deliberately to make people uncomfortable in his presence. Her father took his post behind his desk, looking every bit the authoritarian dictator he wished he were. Derrick remained standing, which gave him that additional position of power. Instead of looking at her, he stared out the window. *Prick.*

She sucked in a deep breath and marshaled her nerves. *Come on gang. Once more with feeling.* "Look. I'm sorry. But you saw the client—they don't care about being the cool kids. They care about authenticity. No offense intended, Derrick, but your presentation would have lost them." She drew in a breath. "Next time I'll follow your direction, but clients like this need a plan they can get behind. They're slow and steady comic-book readers. They don't care about the latest cool-kid party."

Derrick didn't even wait for her father to speak, nor did he face her. "There won't be a next time, Jaya."

"What?" Her eyes burrowed on her father's face. Impassive. But was that really a surprise? "Okay, look, bench me for the next few months if you want, but I'm the best presenter you have. I—"

Derrick turned from his position at the enormous floor to ceiling windows overlooking San Diego's skyline. "No. Not for a few months. Forever."

Jaya's anger simmered to life. But instead of its low-grade burn, it roared to five-alarm status. She turned her gaze on her father. "Dad?" Derrick didn't have the authority to fire her. She still had more shares in the company than he did. Until, of course, he married Tamara.

Her father said nothing for a long moment, the barest hint of exhaustion in his features. "There's a position in accounting if you would prefer. It would be a better fit. I think—"

Jaya blinked. "Did you just say 'accounting'? Dad. I'm not an accountant. I'm an event planner. This is who I am."

He sighed and slid a glance to Derrick. "Then I'm sorry. You leave me no choice. You're fired."

A hazy buzzing sound filled her ears as her father's mouth moved. Disbelief weakened her knees and shock numbed her. *So. Not. Happening.* Her inner fixer took over from her brain because clearly her grey matter was on vacation.

Sure, she'd deviated a little from the original presentation, but not enough to warrant his firing her. Derrick's fast and loose presentation would have had their eyes glazing over.

Her father's voice was tight and low and sounded like gravel being put through a grinder. "We're trying to move Trudeaux forward. The kinds of clients and presentations we want to do will bring us to the next level. Derrick is right. Since you refuse to keep up, you no longer belong at Trudeaux."

She would not cry. "I gave a good presentation." Even as the weak words spilled out, she wondered why she'd bothered. *That was it?* That was her big flare of rebellion? No wonder her father treated her like Carrot Top's ugly twin sister. She couldn't even rebel properly.

Papa Dearest's eye did the twitch-and-jive routine again. "Good presentation? It would have been great if Derrick or Tamara had done it. They both have the vision. We've been preparing for months." His voice rose by increments.

Tears stung her eyes. This wasn't real. It was a dream. Absolutely. Was. Not. Happening. "I just gave you the presentation of my life. You can't just fire me."

When her father spoke again, only the barest hint of his New Orleans accent tinted his baritone. "Jaya, it's done. You're too invested. Too stuck in your ways. Like Derrick was saying, we need to move forward." He cleared his throat, looking momentarily uncomfortable. "This is business, Jaya. I expect you not to be so childish as to skip your sister's wedding in two weeks. We are still a family."

Fuck. Family her ass. This was real? Like they were really telling her to pack up her Weitzman's and bounce? Then expected her at the bloody wedding? Waves of failure and dread braided themselves into a nausea cocktail. She could feel the tension in her neck as if someone was squeezing it tight.

Throat burning from lack of oxygen, she stared at her father. Without a word, he got up from his desk, thin frame moving with a fluidity and grace that belied his age. He left the office with a soft click of his door, Jaya felt more alone than she'd ever felt in her life. Her father had abandoned her.

Derrick spoke and at first Jaya couldn't hear him for the muffled silencer of dread cocooning her. Through the hazy fog of bitter anger and hazy fear, she noticed his mouth moving. The sound coming in slow and lazy increments, as if it didn't matter what else he had to say to her.

"Jaya? Jaya, are you listening?"

She blinked up at him, the urge to strike him so strong she could feel her hand twitch of its own volition. *Oh, God.* She could see the headlines in the Union Tribune. "Angry Black Woman Shoves Ex-Fiancé Through Thirty Story Window." She forced a breath.

Derrick spoke again. His voice tight and in control. "I'll have security pack your things and a messenger deliver them to your apartment before week's end."

Suddenly too exhausted to breathe, she stood on wobbly legs. "Congratulations. You got what you wanted. Are you happy now?"

"You know I don't like seeing your father unhappy. You did this to yourself." He sniffed. "You could have turned this train around any time you liked. You chose to be an adversary."

Before she exited the office, she turned back to glare at him. "You must really hate me." She shrugged. "That's okay because the feeling is mutual."

Jaya managed to hold off the tears until she was down the hall, but then her resolve crumbled and hot wetness streaked down her cheeks. *Come on girl. Suck it up. Or at least wait 'til the elevator.* Getting fired was so not at the top of her "Things To Do Before Hitting Thirty" list. The last thing she needed was to run into her sister or her father before she could get out of the building.

Never let them see you cry. But her stupid tear ducts revolted. She punched the elevator button and wrapped her arms around her ribs in an effort to hold herself together. The chime of the elevator made her wince with its cheery tinkle. The tears on revolt swam into her field of vision like soldiers through a barricade, temporarily blinding her. She forced her leaden legs onto the elevator desperate to get out of the building.

She swiped at the free-falling tears and walked into a wall of muscle.

ONE

For the first time in his life, Alec Danthers had no idea what to do with a woman in his arms. He'd meant to steady and set her away from himself, but her scent struck him. Vanilla and roses. Not overpowering. More like someone baked something delicious while roses opened up in a vase nearby. She smelled like home. Or rather, what he always envisioned home should smell like.

It took him a moment to register her tears. She didn't make a single sound, but he could feel the wet droplets through his shirt. Maybe if she'd been more hysterical, he'd have given her the awkward pat on the back and made his escape on the next available floor.

Like every other male of the species, he had an aversion to a woman's tears. They usually made him feel powerless and lost. But there was something so strong in her silence and in the way she held it all in, only letting the tears and a small shiver escape. Too stunned to do anything else, he wrapped his arms around her shaking frame, but not before pushing the elevator's stop button, figuring she could use a minute.

Every protective instinct made him want to shield her and destroy whatever or whoever had made her cry. In the silence of the elevator, only broken by the soft jazz in the background, he let her cry. He rubbed small circles in her back, whispering hushed nonsense words. The kind muttered by mothers to toddlers with scraped boo-boos. Not that he knew anything about that. His mother wasn't exactly the kissing boo-boos type. But he saw the action performed in enough movies to do a reasonable facsimile. As he rubbed, the long, thick strands of her hair tickled the back of his hand.

Eventually, he felt her deep inhale and she stepped away from him. Every nerve and cell in his body screamed at the loss, but he let her go. She wasn't his to hold on to. But whatever had driven her to cry in the arms of a complete stranger, he'd known pain like that before.

"Holy shit. I'm so sorry," she said, delicate brows drawn down. Her voice, though feminine, was strong. No hint of a waver or a quiver. And it struck him stupid. His whole being responding to it as if she'd stroked him. Skin itchy and tight, he swayed a little. *Whoa.*

"I can't believe I just did that." She spoke again—seemingly unaware she'd had any effect on him.

She hadn't raised her eyes to his, but he knew when she did, there would be no more tears in them, save the ones that clung stubbornly to her lashes instead of rolling down her cheeks.

He cleared his throat, trying to get a mental handle on his brain and body. "It's not a problem. It happens."

She spoke a mile a minute then, words blending together in a stream of consciousness. "Not to me, it doesn't." Her hands flew to cover her cheeks. "I've completely ruined your shirt." She swiped at the drying tears and make-up stains. He held on to the hiss of not-quite-pain as her fingertips brushed at his collar. He forced his jaw shut like a steel bear trap to keep himself from saying anything stupid or groaning in bliss.

"Way to go, Jaya." She shook her head, covering her eyes with her hands. Sucking in a breath, she pulled herself up to full height, which put her forehead at his mouth. She dropped her delicate hands to her sides and muttered another apology. "I'm sorry. I'll pay for the dry-cleaning on your shirt. God." She shook her head again, fumbling for something inside her pocket. When she pulled out a card and proffered it, she leveled her full gaze on him. Almond-shaped, hazel eyes now clear of tears bore into his soul and for the first time in a long time, he felt stripped naked. He saw everything she felt in that honest and open gaze. *Hoooly shit.*

Too much. The pain, the flicker of interest, the embarrassment. Everything she felt came right out in those beautiful eyes. Unused to that kind of honesty from anyone, Alec was torn between falling into her gaze and going into full retreat. She scared the shit out of him. One more glance from her and he'd tell her every secret he ever had.

More than eager to get out of the elevator, he impatiently jabbed at the button to his required floor. Under no circumstances would he call her.

She was a complication he didn't have time for. *Get in and get out, Alec.* He would fix this current mess and be back on a plane to South Africa for the Durban Race in a few weeks. The car was all ready and he pulled a lot of strings to be allowed on that racing team, despite his amateur status. He didn't do knight-in-shining-armor-gigs. *Get out of her presence before you promise her your life or undying loyalty or some shit.* "It's okay."

He peeked down at the card. *Jaya Trudeaux*. "Jaya." He liked the way her name sounded on his tongue.

She blinked up at him, as if surprised to hear him use her name. Then the barest hint of a smile peeked out, showing off even teeth. "You do a lot of these rescue missions? You seem very at ease, considering."

He felt the smile tugging at his lips. "Well, I really had nowhere else to go." He looked around. "Sort of trapped."

"With a crazy crying lady."

He inclined his head. "Somehow I doubt anyone would ever have the nerve to call you crazy."

She looked down at her hands. "You'd be surprised." She shook her head, as if trying to dislodge a vision or memory. "Thanks for the shoulder...." Her voice trailed off.

"Alec."

She closed her eyes. Muttered something like, "It figures," under her breath and stepped to the side, the way people did when they first entered an elevator. His brain searched for something to say, aware that any time he had with her was slipping by with the passing of each floor.

"Will you be okay?"

"You don't have to worry about me. I'm fine. I'm always fine." She gave him a sheepish smile. "Well, except for just now. So maybe if you could forget it ever happened..."

"Consider it forgotten."

Of all the women to stir something awake in him. Talk about inconvenient. In their five-minute interaction, she made him think about parts of himself he hadn't thought about in years. The parts that wanted to get close and to comfort. The parts he knew better than to trust. They stirred within him, wanting to take care of this woman with the wide caramel eyes that made him think of Bambi. *Keep it casual Danthers. Before you get stung.* "Well, whatever it is, I promise you, it's not worth your tears. You can do better."

Alec stumbled off the elevator, feeling like he'd been poleaxed. He whipped his head around as he searched for a floor number. He'd been so eager to escape her, he hadn't paid any attention. Maybe it was the quiet strength with which she held herself together. So strong, she didn't dare show anyone any vulnerability. And when she had, she'd only done so because she was too far gone to keep it together. She reminded him of the only woman he ever loved. *Adele.*

He paused in the middle of the hallway, earning him a quizzical look from the maid. He tried for a charming smile but knew he fell short when she raised an eyebrow. "Sorry. Do you know the way to the Grand Terrace?"

She nodded toward the door he passed on the left. "Next floor up."

He mumbled a thank you and headed for the doorway, taking the stairs two at a time. *Get your head together.* Adele called him home because she needed him. He couldn't afford to have his brain on frappe.

His stepmother spotted him before he even made it out the terrace doors. The smirk on her face tipped up one corner of her lips, making her look younger than her fifty years. She dismissed her assistant in characteristic Adele fashion, with a scowl and a boot up the ass.

Alec tried to hide his chuckle. "Do you have to be so hard on your assistants? That one looked ready to piss herself or jump off the terrace."

She shrugged elegant shoulders. "I need one made of sterner stuff. I don't know why these twenty-something young things keep showing up, hoping I'll teach them how to be a socialite. I expect them to work. Shit, at their age, I already had my own company." She shook her head and scrutinized him. "How's my boy?"

Some of his frozen annoyance at being summoned defrosted a little. She always referred to him as hers. Even though she was his stepmother, she'd treated him like family from the first day he showed up on her doorstep, demanding to see a father he'd never met. It was the sole reason he was standing here now.

"Your boy's fine."

"Bullshit." She placed her hands on her hips, sauntering to the railing like the fashion model she'd once been. "Is it a woman?"

How the hell did she guess? "Nope." Shoving his hands in his pockets, he joined her at the rail.

She faced him, arms stretched out for a hug. He enveloped her in an embrace and wondered how in the world he ever thought her to be a giant. But then and now, she was a force to be reckoned with. Even the hug she gave him was fierce and tight, as if she could take on all his problems. He returned it. *Mom.* The word went unspoken, but both of them knew he how he felt.

She set him away from her and sniffed. "Let me look at you properly. Then we'll talk and maybe you'll tell me about the woman who has you in knots."

"I told you, there's no woman."

"And I'm telling you not to lie to me."

In a hurry to change the subject, he said, "So, what's my little brother done now?"

She wrinkled her brow. "Don't say it like that."

"Come on. I wouldn't be here unless you needed me to

clean up one of his messes. And it would have to be a pretty big mess if I'm here. Normally your lawyers handle it."

She sighed. A deep sigh that told of her age and exhaustion. "It's more than one thing. I don't even know where to begin." She reached out and touched his arm. "I wouldn't place this burden on you if it wasn't important."

He hated that word. *Burden.* He owed her his life. They both knew it. But he wasn't home out of any obligation. He was here for her. Because in all the years of running away from himself, she'd been the only constant.

"As you know, our plan is to go public with Westhorpe, Inc. next year. Until then, we need to keep our noses clean. Stay out of the news, that sort of thing."

"How clean are we talking here?"

"Suffice it to say pristine isn't good enough."

Alec folded his arms over his chest. "So you need me to keep little brother's nose clean? Honestly, Mimi, you could have your security guys do that."

She smiled at the use of his childhood nickname for her before she spoke. "I also need someone to look at the financials for the hotel and the hotel clubs. Synthesis has its grand opening tonight, and I don't want the same kind of losses I've been seeing at the other hotel clubs. To make the San Diego Westhorpe our flagship, we need the full hotel experience—Five Star restaurant, full-to-the-brim nightclub, and the ultimate in luxury hotel. With that model, our books should be in fantastic shape. But I've got accounts not adding up. It was Max's job to look into this and considering he's not here to do it, I wanted someone who's part bloodhound, part business wunderkind and all discreet."

"Get someone else to do it. I'm not the guy for the job. You need someone who's responsible. I'm the black sheep, remember?" If he left tonight, he could be back in Durban in a day.

"Only in your mind. I have my suspicions about why my hotels are losing money. I need you to verify them."

"You want Max for this. Not me." Where the hell had his brother run to? "Did you check the usual places?" Max taking off wasn't something new. Why Adele wanted him back so badly was the real note of interest. "You don't need me to find him. You can hire many a private investigator. Better yet, hire Caleb Atkins. He's got a whole security team that does nothing but solve corporate security issues." And it never hurt to throw his best friend some work.

"It's a little more complicated this time." She paused to fiddle with a flower arrangement on the table. "I'm sure you remember Sue Wentz, your former girlfriend. Well, she's pregnant, and Maxwell has run away from his responsibility."

Sue. Pregnant? By Max? This was a round of deja vu he could do without. His mind's eye filled with the image of the strawberry blonde girl with the kind eyes he thought he loved once. From the start he knew they weren't a good match, but he tried to give her what she wanted. In the end, he made them both unhappy.

Clearing his throat, he said, "Mimi, this is a family dispute. They need to work things out on their own."

"You know he's spiraling out of control. I need you to help me stop it. The board gave me two weeks to bring him back and handle the situation of our books."

"Still not my problem." Alec needed to get out of Dodge before she roped him in. He rocked back on his heels.

"Do you at least care that he drained his trust fund?"

TWO

AFTER THREE DAYS, JAYA STILL COULDN'T PULL HERSELF out of the fog. Whenever she thought of getting up and actually getting dressed, her brain reminded her she had nowhere to go and she plunged back into the paralyzed pit of despair. She knew the situation was dire when her usual cadre of bad action movies couldn't cheer her up.

Cracking an eyelid open, she surveyed the wasteland that was her apartment. The urge to vomit came on strong. Chinese food cartons, empty ice-cream cartons, empty chocolate wrappers—the mess was so bad, she returned to hiding under her cover, where it was safer.

The buzzer to her front door rang. She ignored it. Cue the cavalry. Maybe if she pretended she didn't hear them, they'd go away. She'd managed to avoid her two best friends Ricca Munroe and Micha Bennett for the past several days, but it was only a matter of time before they insisted on seeing her. "You're going to have to pick the lock if you want in," she shouted, popping her head out from underneath the duvet.

"You're not really daring me, are you, Trudeaux?"

For a moment, Jaya worried about her lock. Micha had all manner of skills and Jaya didn't know if lock-picking was one of them. She eyed the door with dubious concern. Deadbolts couldn't be picked, could they? "Go away. I'm not accepting visitors."

"You might be old money from New Orleans, but I don't take orders from you. Now open the damn door."

"There's no need to shout," Ricca said in a hushed tone.

"Thank you for coming, but I am not opening the door. I'm wallowing. Deep wallowing going on. No guests invited to this wallowing party."

Silence. Maybe they'd taken the hint. The sunlight streaming in from her balcony fought a valiant battle with her duvet cover, but her tugging and securing of the blanket around her won the fight in the blanket's favor and no light streamed into her self-imposed cave. Nausea and dread threaded through her belly.

This was all wrong. Every romantic comedy movie ever made had their heroines feeling better after gorging on ice-cream and shopping themselves stupid. Leave it to her to feel sick at the evidence of both her attempts. She couldn't even look at the bag she'd left by her front door. Who the hell tried to soothe a bruised ego with three-thousand-dollar shoes?

There was some shuffling at the door. *Damn, those chicks are persistent.* It was, of course, the reason they were friends in the first place. *Never say die.* And if you do say die, make sure it's with fabulous footwear and you take a piece of someone with you.

Her heart lurched into overdrive as the bolt disengaged. She yanked the covers off her head in time to see Micha saunter in with a triumphant grin, jangling a set of keys in her hand. "You know, you really should tell Marco and his fine ass not to give keys to any old bitch who smiles and flashes some tit at him. By the way, I still insist you need to do him before he heads back to Brazil this summer. That is too much hotness for one of us not to take a crack at."

The doorman had given them the key? *Traitor*. Micha was right—that Brazilian piece of hotness couldn't help himself for a pretty smile. But she wasn't going to sleep with him. No matter how much he made her blush every time he said her name in his accented English.

Ricca followed close behind Micha. Her smile, though, was laced with concern. It only got worse as she caught a load of the mess in Jaya's living room.

Micha took charge. "Ree, you get her brown booty into the shower. I'll start cleaning up this dump."

Feeling mutinous, Jaya folded her limbs Indian style. "I don't need a shower. Nor do I need you to come into *my* house and boss me around. What if I like my place looking like this?" She darted a glance around. Pigsty was a gross under-exaggeration. The old her didn't handle mess well. The new-unemployed-loser her didn't give a shit.

Even Ricca had to snort. "Come on, honey. I'm surprised you're not at the rug with a dust-buster already. Let's go. I'll wrap your hair up so you can get in the shower."

Jaya scowled. "Shit, do I smell that bad?"

Micha nodded as Ricca shook her head, but only Micha spoke. "Did you know you have an ice-cream smear on one of your boobs?"

Jaya's head snapped down, then back up again to look at her friends. *Goddamn*. She *was* a mess.

A look of mock alarm crossed over Micha's face. "If you're going to cry, take it outside. No pussies in my camp."

Jaya barked out a laugh. "Yeah, hard-ass. I get you." Giving Ricca her best I'm-a-pathetic-chick-so-don't-hold-it-against-me smile, she added. "Lead the way."

After she showered, she'd changed her ice-cream-stained sweatshirt for jeans and a graphic T-shirt that read "My balls are bigger than yours." The way she figured, she could use the extra boost of confidence.

When she went back to the living room, the tornado was over and her friends were staring at the bag containing the evidence of the need to self-soothe. "I did a little shopping."

"We can see that." Ricca's breath came out in little puffs of air.

Both she and Micha stared at the bag with envy and wonder. Self-conscious, Jaya muttered, "Don't worry, I can return it."

Micha frowned, but her eyes were alive and excited. "I know a Gold's Boutique sale bag when I see one. The pink ribbon means you got this on sale, and that means there's no turning back. What did you buy?"

"Fine. But I'll have you know I'm not proud of myself. And I'll be forced to sell myself on El Cajon Boulevard in order to pay for these." Jaya pulled out the simple shoe box. Just the name on the box had Ricca stumbling back.

"Oh, Jaya. You didn't."

Heat crept up Jaya's collarbone. "Unfortunately, I did."

Speechless, Micha's fingers reached out and caressed the outside of the black box. Jaya knew how she felt. The temptation to put on the shoes and run around without a care was strong. Nestled in pretty pick tissue wrapping were the latest pair of Christian Louboutin stilettos. Shimmery gold with hints of red. Stunning. Absolutely stunning. The three of them had eyed them on a shopping trip a month ago. None had dared even look at the price tag.

Micha plopped herself on the couch. "I gotta tell you, getting fired is a big deal but doesn't warrant pocketbook suicide."

"I already feel rotten enough." She recounted the whole story of the firing.

Ricca growled. "That stupid asshole is worth less than Satan's left nut. I'm going to kill him *and* your father. Of all the bullshit in the world, this has got to be the biggest pile."

Jaya could only stare. Ricca didn't lose her temper. That was Micha's job. Micha tearing off was just Micha being Micha. Ricca tearing off was something to be feared.

Ricca touched her hand and squeezed. Warm brown eyes glistened with sympathy tears. "We're here for you. If you want, I can see if we've got an opening at Fantasies. You know you'd be a shoo-in with your experience and reputation."

She would not cry. She would not cry. She would not—*Well damn.* The splash of a hot tear had Jaya hanging her head. She'd actually failed. And now the people who she loved most in the world were witness to her failure.

As Jaya lifted her head, she heaved a deep sigh. When her eyes met Micha's, her friend's eyes were soft, kind and a little shimmery. What the—? Was Micha crying for her?

Micha stood, swiftly taking the shoes with her. She kept her back to the two of them. Clearing her throat, she picked up one of the shimmery gold shoes and said, "Jesus. They're gorgeous. But you can't keep them."

"I know." Jaya eyed the shoes in Micha's hands. "How could something so beautiful be so awful?"

Micha shook her head. "Well, you're not the first woman to lose control with the credit card when things get a little rocky. No feeling sorry for yourself. Solution time."

Ricca gnawed delicately on a fingernail. "Well maybe we could Craigslist them."

Both Jaya and Micha shouted no, then giggled.

Finally Jaya said, "No. They're too beautiful for Craigslist. Besides, I would only get a fraction of what they're worth."

"Fine." Ricca breathed. "Then I have a solution, but Micha's going to have to agree to it too."

"What?" Jaya eyed her dubiously. "If it involves becoming a shake-your-booty-ho to pay for them, I'm not interested."

Ricca rolled her eyes and giggled. "How about we share the shoes?" Jaya frowned, but Ricca continued as if she hadn't noticed. "We borrow everything from each other already. Why not do a footwear time-share?"

"Which means," Micha said as she paused to caress the gold strap, "you're only out a grand."

Jaya's jaw unhinged. There was no way. "Wait, I can't let you bail me out like that. I'm the moron who let my credit card act as my brain with no job or sugar daddy. I can't make you suffer the consequences too."

Micha ignored her outrage and continued stroking the shoe. "Who's suffering?" She pulled the shoe in closer and admired the detailing. "I'd drop six hundred dollars easy on a pair." She shrugged "Not too bright, but we've all done something stupid in the name of retail therapy before. And like you said, these are an investment. Some fabulously insane Carrie Bradshaw type will pay the big bucks for this pair one day."

"Micha's right. Besides, if I'm going to spend money, what better way than insane footwear and in assistance of a friend?"

Jaya couldn't believe her ears. "You guys would do that for me?"

Both rolled their eyes and nodded.

"Consider yourself my charity event for the week." Micha smirked.

Ricca grinned. "Now. What are you going to wear with these when we go out tonight?"

THREE

Come on, Trudeaux. Shoulders back, chin up. You are amazing. Jaya was well aware of the impact the three of them made in the crowded lounge. They weren't the typical San Diego girls, tall, blonde and leggy—but they were stunning in the way they stood out from the crowd with their brown skin and dark hair. Or at least, she could be made stunning just by standing between her friends. With Ricca's curves and Micha's striking looks and hair, nobody could help but look twice. For once though, she didn't bask secretly in the glow of secondary adoration. But maybe Micha was right. If she faked it, she'd start feeling better.

They selected the booth by the bar. It had easy access to drinks, a great view of the dance floor, and was close to the side exit in case the place was packed and they didn't want to go through the lobby of the Westhorpe Hotel to get out.

Jaya slid into the booth, careful to keep the skirt of her dress bunched. The damn thing was so frothy and flirty, every time she moved, the skirts threatened to lift up and expose her ass to the world. The top was no better. The neckline was so daring, she hadn't bothered to wear a bra with it, putting her goods even more on display. But at least she was comfortable in the shoes. They felt like padded silk and they looked amazing. The perfect complement to the dress.

Once their drinks arrived, Jaya raised her glass as she tried to shake the feeling that someone was watching her. Though, given the Do-Me shoes and the Look-At-Me dress, she should have been more surprised if someone *wasn't* watching her.

"Okay, listen closely, ladies, because this is the only time you'll be hearing this from my mouth. You were right." She paused for effect. "I do feel better. Thanks to you guys, I'm not pulling the death-by-cookies-'n'-cream routine. And—I have a plan."

Ricca raised her glass and clinked it with Jaya's.

Micha's grin was broad as she spoke. "I knew we'd see the old you eventually—Planning and everything. Soon you'll be making one of us a to-do list. You're on the road to recovery." She took a sip of her Lemon Drop, her ruby-red lips closing around the rim of her martini glass. "So, what's the plan? Should I get my shovel? Will this require a trip to the desert and a body burial?"

"As much as I would love to throw Derrick in a ditch, I've got something else in mind." With the hairs on her neck standing at attention and making her take furtive look around, she continued in a softer voice. "I'm going to finish my drink. Then I'm going to get my job back—and oust the interloper from my family."

Micha and Ricca exchanged wide-eyed looks. "I prefer the desert idea," Micha mumbled.

"Well, okay. As soon as I *legally* get rid of him, I'll don the sexiest of cat-burglar-chic and help you dig." Jaya sighed cheerily as she took another sip of her drink. "I will be back on top in no time."

Ricca's happy face went from friendly bolstering to wary concern. "Exactly what *is* the plan?"

A shot of adrenaline zinged through Jaya. Now that she had a strategy, the tension was already rolling out of her shoulders. "First things first. I'm going to get a date to Tamara's wedding. There's no way I can show up alone. It just screams 'I'm a jobless loser who can't even find a boyfriend.'"

Micha slapped the table top. "At last. Now you're talking sense. I told you all that *I'm-strong-enough-to-go-to-the-wedding-alone* nonsense was bullshit."

"Yes, you were right. There's no way I want to show up alone." She shrugged. "Besides, it won't hurt to have somebody hot as a fixture. Someone who won't think Tamara is the most beautiful woman on the planet and the sun shines out of her ass."

Micha snickered. "Is *that* what a sunrise looks like?"

Jaya chuckled. "Once I have a date to the wedding, my real work begins. I know for a fact Dad has invited some of our largest clients to the wedding. And I'm sure they'll win the conference bid. When they do, Dad will be beside himself to invite Brett James to it. He loves to schmooze and give an air of family at Trudeaux."

"But how do you plan to get close to him?" Micha asked. "Won't Derrick try and keep you away?"

"Probably. But I'll figure a way around it. I just need to speak with the client. I know I had Brett at that pitch."

"You two are on a first-name basis now?"

Jaya grinned. "You'd better believe it. Once the client starts grumbling that he wants me back on the project, Dad won't have much of a choice but to reinstate me."

Ricca shook her head, sending her glossy black hair waving around her shoulders. "I don't know, Jai. Sounds risky. What if the client doesn't demand to have you back?"

Jaya waved a dismissive hand. "I have that covered. I know this client inside out. I'm a comic-book-reading, superhero-loving, self and publicly professed nerd. They won't want a substitute. I know what I'm doing."

"Okay, so when do we start trolling our contacts for Mr. Perfect?" Micha pulled out her phone, apparently ready to get on the case. "You only have two weeks. And we'll want to help you audition them, shirts off of course." She waggled her eyebrows.

Ricca giggled. "You could always take Beckett Mills."

Jaya shook her head. "No go on Beckett. I've known him since college. It'll be hard to pass him off as my boyfriend, since Dad and Tams know him too. You must have some male model types you use for Fantasies, Inc."

"Yeah, we use an agency. I suppose we could hire you someone. But why pay if you can get a real date?"

Micha tapped her phone. "That'll be our last resort. In the meantime, I have a couple of guys I've been dying to fix you up with."

I've done it now. Now that she'd opened the floodgates, her friends would be all over this.

Through the crowd, she noticed Beckett's broad shoulders making their way over to the booth. Most people got out of his way—something she'd never understand because he was harmless. His blond good looks and lazy countenance should have put people at ease, but instead, he made people nervous. Ricca especially. Maybe it was his eyes. They were shrewd. Never missed anything. That and his six-foot-five build.

As he joined them, Jaya put on her best brave face smile. But he saw right through it. "Cut the shit, Jaya. You're a terrible liar."

She flashed Ricca a look. "Did you tell him? I know you two work together, but is there no loyalty?"

He rolled his eyes. "She didn't have to tell me anything. I called your office. Then your secretary—who's now your sister's secretary, by the way—told me you were fired. What the fuck?"

Jaya cleared her throat. "Yeah, long story. Pretty much the old man lost his mind and I'm out of a gig. Oh, and did I mention I'm still expected at that stupid wedding?"

He winced. "If you want, I—"

She cut him off. "Already been through that. And no. But thanks."

To avoid the uncomfortable shift in emotion, Jaya scanned the crowd. The usual glitterati were out in full force. Short skirts, bleach-blonde hair and teetering heels. Her eyes shifted to the bar area and she froze. *No. It couldn't be.*

Alec. Leaning against the bar. Staring at her. The way she saw it, she had two options. Duck under the table and hide, though not the best choice because, given the skirt, everyone would see the color of her thong. There was the option of shuffling out of the booth and making a break for it. But Micha was quick and Jaya would never make it out without having to explain herself.

As he approached, her whole body tensed, every beat of her heart wearing a more permanent pattern into her chest cavity. *Shit.* With every step he took, he looked like a predator. The sexual approach she could handle. A kind-hearted, hey-aren't-you-the-girl-who-cried-on-my-jacket? thing she couldn't do. If he showed her pity, she'd cry and ruin Micha's excellent makeup job. Not to mention he'd probably think she was crazy for real.

All of his tall, dark and delicious frame paused at their booth. "I got tired of waiting for you to come to the bar, so I figured I'd brave the crowd."

The velvet voice melted into her center making her core contract. The broad chest didn't help either. Talk about a sexy, make-your-panties-drop kind of body. She whipped her head up to meet his gaze.

If anyone asked her later, she would swear up and down she tried to form words—

Intelligent words. Instead, all she managed was the flap-jaw routine. Open, close. Open, close.

"Cat got your tongue?" He grinned at her.

Damn, that smile should be illegal. "I-I—Uh..."

Clutching his hand to his heart, he added on the extra charm. "I'm wounded. It's worse than I feared. You've forgotten my name *and* my face."

The giggle escaped before she could corral it. "I haven't forgotten your name, *Alec*. You're the one who forgot to call me about your shirt."

"Ahh, you remember me then. It's a start. And I did call you. *You* forgot to mention that you no longer worked at Trudeaux Events."

Heat suffused her face. "Well, since they were the reason I ruined your shirt, I figured they should pay."

"And if I told you I didn't call about my shirt?"

Great. A charmer. Derrick had been a charmer once. "I'd say you had no other reason to be calling me." She felt Micha nudge her with her foot.

Alec put his hand over his heart. "Ouch. Shot down by a goddess."

Jaya fought not to roll her eyes. "Does this approach ever work for you? The whole I'm-sexy-and-have-more-charm-than-brains thing?"

"So, you think I'm sexy?" He winked at her. "I'm just going to ignore the rest."

"Are you going to introduce us to your friend, Jai?" Micha made no bones about her open admiration as she eyed Alec up and down. "Even better, is your new friend going to introduce me to his friend at the bar?" Micha turned and waved to the tall man at the bar with the sandy brown hair.

Jaya could feel her skin grow hot. She wasn't supposed to ever see him again. He wasn't supposed to be charming *and* hot. This wasn't supposed to happen. She had a plan to implement. "He's not my friend. He's—"

"Alec Danthers. Ladies," he said with a grin at Ricca and Micha, but only nodded at Beckett. Maybe it was some guy thing, but the two of them didn't speak and Jaya could sense the malevolence coming off Beckett in waves.

Ricca and Micha both traitorously grinned back at him.

"Allow me to buy your drinks for the rest of the evening," he said to them. "Maybe you can put a good word in with your friend for me."

Jaya rolled her eyes. Taking in the badge on his shirt that said Manager, she said, "Isn't it your job to make sure the bar makes money and not loses it?"

"And not hit on my friend?" Beckett grumbled beside her, but no one paid attention to him.

"I think the Westhorpe Hotel can handle a couple of free drinks for some beautiful women."

While Alec chatted with her friends, Jaya realized the carefree flirtation had vanished. Sure, he still smiled and complimented her friends, but something she'd said had turned off the light inside. *Damn.*

"Thanks for the offer of drinks, Alec. But, if you'll excuse me, I'm headed to the dance floor." Walking away she could feel his gaze on her back burning her flesh.

Jaya joined the gyrating throngs on the dance floor and she closed her eyes and moved her body to the tune of Rihanna's "S&M." As Jaya moved her hips to the lyrics about chains and whips, a warm hand landed on her hip. Sharp zips of electricity jolted her flesh.

The deep voice at her ear was low and inviting. "Come see me when you're ready for a drink."

Alec kept his hand on her hip for a moment too long. His parting squeeze made her body yearn for a more intimate touch.

Even as she turned to face him, he had already moved toward the bar. When her friends joined her on the dance floor, she bit back a smile as Micha gave her a clear, girl-go-get-your-man look. Ricca just fanned herself and fake-swooned. Silly girls. Charmers are for morons. And this was not her first trip to the rodeo.

"Honey, if you don't go and get him, I will." Micha booty bumped her. "You put on your moxy—borrow mine if you must —and go make me proud. I'm going to take on his friend."

Jaya turned towards her goal, her body jerking with adrenaline at the thought of her plan. Or maybe that was Micha's shove in Alec's general direction. Either way, Jaya's feet navigated the masses of the pretty and rich towards the promise of some serious sexual gratification. Though, the closer she got to him, she had a feeling she'd been ensnared rather than the one ensnaring.

Taking in his longish dark hair curling at the ends, she wondered how it would feel between her fingertips. Tousled as it was, it gave him a youthful appearance. Those eyes, though. They were by far his best feature. That unusual shade of blue framed by black, sooty lashes. As she openly ogled, she decided his eyes were not his best feature. Strong shoulders, flat stomach. Given the hard planes of his chest when he held her, she was pretty sure his black polo hid a pretty excellent set of abs.

Mr. Sex on a Stick looked just like the panacea she needed. She needed to flirt a little, secure the date, then move on with the plan. She reminded her libido that everything hinged on getting the plan to work right. *Focus. You can do anything.* She just needed to pretend she was a superhero.

When she reached the bar, he grinned at her. "If you'd waited another minute to come over, I'd have found a reason to come to you. I had wingmen standing at the ready to occupy your friends."

Jaya knew she must be blushing, but she held on tight to her borrowed pair of brass balls. "Micha's already secured one of your wingmen." She indicated the dance floor where Micha, pressed up against Alec's friend, worked her hips in time to Sean Paul "I fear for his life. Or his c—."

He barked out a laugh, interrupting her. "Do you always say what's on your mind?" He eyed the pair. "Besides, I think Caleb can keep up."

She liked the feel of the brass balls she wielded, not watching what she said. Not being so cautious. "No. I don't always speak my mind. But I think I'm starting to like it."

He reached out to brush a stray hair from her cheek. The contact had her wobbling in her heels and she placed a hand on his chest to steady herself.

His sharp intake of breath and the hitch in his heartbeat under her hand gave her the final boost of confidence she needed.

Leaning in, she pressed her mouth to his. She pulled back and murmured, "Let's go somewhere."

Those three words zinged around in Jaya's head, repeating over and over and over again. Had she really said that? She slid Alec a look from under her lashes and saw naked lust sprinkled with a pinch of curiosity.

Without a word to her, he took her hand and pulled her around the bar. Tossing a set of keys to the other man behind the bar, he ground out a command. "Lock up."

FOUR

NOT EXACTLY ACCORDING TO PLAN. AS ALEC TOWED JAYA through the back exit of the bar to the VIP elevator, he wondered how he'd gotten here. He'd meant to ask her out. Flirt his way to dinner. Find out who or what had made her cry the other day. But screw his best-laid plans—he wanted her. The ridiculous instinct to protect and possess were driving his actions now.

Tugging her into the elevator, he marveled at how soft her hand was. The charge of electricity zinging up his arm every time he stroked her thumb could be a potential problem. Not like he cared though. As soon as she'd laid those perfect lips on his, rational thought hadn't been part of the plan. Reckless and impulsive—that was his MO. *Just like your father. Just like your brother.*

"Hey, aren't I supposed to be the one frowning?" Jaya met his gaze. A laugh in her eyes, she added, "Strange man drags me to secret hotel entrance. *Hot*, strange man, but strange man none the less. I should be the one having second thoughts."

He couldn't help it. Her impish grin made him smile. From

the moment he saw her in the elevator three days ago, he had had some outrageous fantasies about her lips. How they would feel under his, how they'd look around his—

She moistened her bottom lip with the tip of her tongue and he bit back a strangled moan.

"I'm going to kiss you again now if that's okay."

She greeted him with a smile so wide her eyes danced. "Oh, I think it might be okay."

She did that tip-of-the tongue thing again and his cock jerked. Cupping her face in his hands, he pressed his mouth to hers, meaning to be gentle. Instead, he felt like he had electrodes molded to his lips, sending electric currents of need through his body. *Shit.* He heard her moan and dragged her closer to him, unable, unwilling to break their contact.

His tongue coaxed a response, demanding more. When her tongue answered and met his, need slammed into his body with such force, he thought he might come. *Holy shit, it's just a kiss.* But his body didn't believe that. He wanted her so badly his blood boiled. As their tongues danced, he lifted her so her legs wrapped around him. He fisted his hands in her hair and could feel the heat from her core. Her soft moans urged him on—to take, plunder. *Quick, hard. Fast.*

The elevator dinged and she drew back. Her tone was light, curious. "You going to tell me where you're taking me, or are you going to ravage, then slaughter me in the elevator?"

He eased her down his body. The moment they broke contact, he missed her. "I like the sound of this ravaging business. But if you really must see your surroundings first, then let me show you around."

Once he led her into Max's suite, she used his arm to steady herself as she slipped off her shoes. The mental image of her wearing nothing but the stilettos would give him wet dreams for a month.

"Where are we, anyway?"

"One of the presidential suites." Alec kept his voice neutral. Jaya wouldn't be the first girl to be impressed with the Westhorpe trappings. It was the reason he never brought women home, why he never told anyone he was a Westhorpe.

She stared up at the ornate painted ceiling done in the fashion of Botticelli paintings. "It's beautiful. This paint color is gorgeous."

"If you like that sort of thing." To his own ears, his voice was rueful and a little bitter.

"It reminds me of my parent's house. Gorgeous, but stifling. Like the room wasn't really meant to be enjoyed."

The relief that washed through him was so potent he thought he'd collapse from it. His first impressions of her were right. She went her own way. She wasn't up here with him because she knew who he was. She didn't care about the money. Or she didn't know. Either way, she'd come up with Alec Danthers not Alec Westhorpe.

Jaya turned a slow circle in the middle of the room. The soft skirt of her dress lifted and teased him with hints of her upper thighs. "Are we supposed to be up here, Alec?"

He shrugged. "Define 'supposed to be.'"

A smile threatened but she restrained it. "I've always wondered if hotel employees used the unoccupied rooms for their own dirty deeds. I guess now I know. I don't want you to get into any trouble, though." She took in the furnishings again. "At least you picked a good one. I'm getting all kinds of ideas in here."

He nearly swallowed his tongue. *Shit.* Clearing his throat, he said, "It's my brother's place. I stay here with him when I'm in town."

"Fancy," she muttered. Jaya stalked toward him and he wondered how the tables had turned. He started out seducing her, but somehow she was in control here. She was in the driver's seat. The thought made him itchy.

"So," she said as she approached, "I guess the only thing I need to know is if he's coming back tonight and how much time we have."

Alec's smile spread into an all-out grin. An unseen fist tightened in his belly. "I gotta tell you. I love a woman who goes after what she wants." His voice was rough as he ground the words out.

Backing her against the wall of the sitting area, he braced himself for the shot of electricity bolting through his veins. But when he dipped his head and their lips met, her return kiss was so tender it had him on slow melt. While his lips glided over hers in curious exploration, her tongue teased and coaxed his.

Hard and fast was what he wanted—or thought he wanted. He'd gone looking for a flash of heat. His body hadn't bargained for this kind of slow and easy kissing as if they had all the time in the world and he was a fine wine to be savored.

Heat spread from the center of his body, rising to the epidermis and scorching his skin from the inside. Breath trapped in his throat, he tried to speed up the pace. The slow torture was telling him everything he needed to know about her. She was thorough. Took her time. Didn't rush things. She liked to be in control. It also meant she was confident and strong.

Sexy didn't even begin to cover it. Good thing he was leaving soon. A woman like Jaya would shred his soul. He could see himself giving her anything she asked for. Including his freedom.

If she kept the slow burn up any longer, he would become a believer in spontaneous combustion. Alec heard a low rumbling in the quiet of the room. It wasn't until he felt her smile against his lips that he realize he was the source.

Without breaking their kiss, he slid his hands down her arms and brought them up to wrap around the back of his neck. He mumbled nonsense words more focused on getting her as close to him as physically possible. One kiss had reduced him to a horny teenager and his brain couldn't compute.

Looking down at her, feeling her warmth around him, the soft curves of her body gently molded against him, he couldn't remember his own name. Couldn't think beyond what he wanted. Couldn't think beyond the need slamming through his chest.

Jaya arched her body into him and smiled. He couldn't remember why he'd ever thought it was a good idea to stay away from her. As he kissed her again, he thought he was branding her as his, but really it was the other way around. Jaya Trudeaux stripped him bare. She made him feel. "You are so beautiful."

In the tiniest corner of his mind, a voice called to him to be careful. It tried to warn him that she was dangerous to him. That he wouldn't be able to leave her easily as he did with so many others before. That she wasn't his. But he didn't listen. All he could hear were her ragged pants. All he could think about were those full lips and where he wanted them. How much he wanted her to be his.

He didn't realize he'd pulled back and was staring at her until big honey-brown eyes blinked up at him as if waiting for some sort of command. The sweet and spicy scent of perfume mingled with her scent. He leaned his body into hers. He knew something inside him would change forever if he did this. He had a choice—listen to the voice, or fall into those brown depths. *Voice or depths. Voice or depths.* Tilting his head, sliding his lips over hers, he chose depths.

She tasted like autumn. The flavor of apple mojito mingled with her unique brown sugar flavor. Hands tightening on her waist, Alec nipped at her bottom lip and she responded to him with a shiver. Her response made his cock jump up and threaten war with the fly of his jeans.

With every breath, shift and wiggle from her, he could feel the heat of her through his fly. He traced a path to her neck, inhaling deeply. She arched into him, pressing those full breasts into his chest. Needing to feel more of her, he slid a hand up to the V of her dress. Tracing the material as it clung to the rise of one perfect mound, he heard her sharp intake of breath and watched with fascination as her nipple puckered under the stretchy jersey fabric. No bra. *Shit.*

Continuing to trace his finger at the edge of the fabric, he used the other hand to restrain both of hers above his head. She didn't struggle, only rocked her heat against him. Taking advantage of her arched form, he hovered his mouth for a moment over the puckered bud. He blew a warm breath and she shivered again as her body arched even more.

Not one to disappoint a lady, he pressed his lips over the raised peak and suckled her through the soft material. Her breath came out as a drawn out moan and he tugged harder trying to taste every rich flavor of her skin through the fabric.

Letting go of her hands, his fingers trembled as they peeled back the shoulders of the dress. One simple tug and it skimmed off her shoulders to her waist, baring the blackberry tinted tips of her breasts. Another tug and the dress slid to the polished travertine of the floor. Gaze still on hers, he slid his hands to her hips, looped his thump in her thong, then tugged down. Only then, did he step back to admire the view. *Shit*. Perfection.

Alec's brain stuttered. She was more perfect than the goddess Nefertiti herself. It had been a long time since anyone affected him. Since any woman had touched more than just his flesh. Jaya had managed it the moment he saw her. And now. Now she stood before him in all her naked perfection and his mind completely fuzzed out on what to do.

Lucky for him, she knew what she wanted. "Alec, I need this." She gazed up at him through thick lashes. "I need you."

Alec couldn't move. He'd had sex—lots of sex. Shit, he'd had all sorts of sex on six different continents. Never once had he felt truly connected. Not like he did now. Jaya reached for him and he could only watch as delicate fingers tugged his cotton polo out of his pants. She leaned in close commingling her scent with his.

Her hands, delicate, but sure, moved inside the shirt, skimming his shoulders as she slipped it off over his head. At the contact of skin on skin, his cock pressed against his pants, urging, begging him to love her. To slide into her soft warm depths and never come back up for air.

Heat flared in Jaya's eyes as his cock nudged her belly. As he felt the now-familiar shock of electricity, he eased her hands away from his belt. He grabbed a foil packet from his wallet before violently kicking off his pants. Alec left the boxer briefs on, tucking the condom in the waistband at his back.

For a moment, he saw the look of confusion in her eyes. His body finally surging into motion, he shifted her onto the antique end desk, slanting over her lips again like a starving man.

His hands took their cue from the roaring, pulsing blood in his veins and slid over her hips to her rounded ass. Cupping her flesh, he levered her against him. "Put your legs around my waist."

When she complied, he cursed as her wet heat met the cloth covering the head of his straining penis. He braced her against the corner and slowed the kiss. Taking his time, he teased her tongue into dancing with his.

He traversed a path from her full ass to her waist to her breasts, never quite reaching the sensitive tips. Jaya moaned and rocked against him trying to get closer, urging him to take her breasts in his hands. When he gave her what she wanted, she moaned and arched her back, giving him better access.

Those breasts were a thing of beauty. He'd always been an ass man and Lord knew Jaya had one that could win awards, but her breasts were quickly making him a breast man. They weren't much bigger than a B-cup, but they were high and firm —and real. For some reason most of the women he slept with these days sported fakes.

Jaya arched her back as much as the confined space would allow. He took the hint. Dipping his head, he grazed first one nipple, then the other with his five o'clock shadow. He followed up with his tongue and with playful tugs with his teeth.

"Alec."

He wanted to hear her moan again.

He growled against her breast. "I like it when you say my name."

She said it again on a whisper and he sucked in a delicate tip. One arm wrapped around her for support, he slid his hand down the flat expanse of her belly. Only pausing to trace a circle around her belly button, his hand slid farther down, searching for her center.

When he found it, he hissed in a breath. She was wet. Slick. Teasing the entrance, he slid one finger into her moist core and she bucked. He buried his lips in her neck, inhaling the scent of her. She smelled like home. Gently, he withdrew then entered, withdrew, then entered in a slow, lazy rhythm that said they had all the time in the world. When in truth, they only had a minute before he spontaneously combusted.

Her hands fisted in his hair and she rocked her hips against his finger, trying to force him to increase the pace. He didn't. Instead, he inserted another finger and kept up the rhythm. *Nice and easy.* They had all the time in the world.

Jaya raked her nails up his back and he chuckled through a hiss. "You're making it really hard for me to take my time."

Doing it again, she asked, "Who said I wanted you to take your time?"

Hell. If that didn't wreak havoc with his self-control. Easing his fingers out of her, he reached around his back for the condom. With a series of wiggles, his briefs went the way of her dress. Getting the condom on in their current position took more effort than he thought, but when he was sheathed and his cock nudged her slick folds, he didn't care. All he could think about was how she felt against him.

"Alec, now."

Her rocking motions caused her sex to rub against his tip.

He shuddered from the need. "I'll go easy."

She smiled. "There you go, trying to make decisions for me again. When I want easy, I'll ask for it."

With slow, tilting motions of his hips, he slid in to the hilt.

They both hissed in breaths. Hers was an "Ahhhhh." His "Ohhhhh."

Bliss. He rocked his hips back, slowly pulling out, and rocked forward again. As his cock stocked the sensitive walls of her flesh, she dug her nails deep, scoring marks a part of him hoped would become permanent.

She tossed her head back, baring her neck to him. Taking advantage, he nipped at the column of her neck even as he drew forward and the sensitive flesh of her core milked his cock. Pulsing and releasing in its tight sheath.

"Alec." His name on her breath was both a balm to the part of him that was always searching, always moving, and an accelerant to the driving urge for self-destruction. Even as their bodies moved together, mixing sweat and her perfume, Alec knew once wouldn't be enough. She was already under his skin. As he drove her higher and higher and felt the tingling at the base of his spine, he knew walking away from Jaya Trudeaux would be torture.

"Alec. Please." Her delicate fingers twined in his hair, pulling him close.

"Come on, sweetheart." He drove into her with a demanding pace. No longer coaxing, but demanding she be his for a night. For a millennium. "I want to feel you around my cock as you come. Let go, Jaya. You're safe with me."

"I—" Her breath hitched.

He ground his teeth together. The tingle in his spine had turned into fire. He couldn't hold back. "Jaya."

Her body trembled in his arms and he felt the quiver of her slick flesh against his cock. "Oh. Fuck. Me."

As she came, her body flooded his and clamped tight around

him, unwilling to let him go. The last thought he had before his body jerked in heated relief was *home*.

DARKNESS. That's all Jaya's brain registered. She blinked her eyes. Nope, still darkness. She rolled over under the duvet to try and get a glimpse at her bedside clock. Instead, an arm flung around her waist, bringing her up against a wall of muscle and... erm, yeah, that was definitely someone's penis. Someone's hard, thick penis pressing against her hip.

Shit. Her brain began a frantic scramble for purchase. She dragged in a breath, smelled spices and mint, and smiled. *Alec*. The muscles of her lower belly contracted and the tingles in her belly made her bite her lip. She could feel her body soften for him. Achy inner thighs fell apart in anticipation. Put that all together and what do you have—Get the hell out of Dodge time.

Peeling the heavy arm off her waist, she tried to orient herself. Maybe this was all a dream. Maybe if she pinched herself, she'd wake up in her own bed. Except her brain flooded with memories of her fingers laced in dark curly hair as he licked her to a toe-curling orgasm. More images of her straddling and riding strong hips as his electric blue eyes worshiped her body. The final image of her with hands braced against the French doors of the balcony while he took her from behind. Alec + Alec + Alec equaled So. Totally. Screwed.

Jaya slapped her hands over her flushed face. What the hell had she been thinking, sleeping with Elevator Guy? She'd bought in to Micha's whole moxy pep talk. Stupid, stupid, stupid. More stupid if she just lay here, waiting for Mr. I'm a

Sex God to wake up. Awkward post coital—make that multiple coitals morning-after seshes—were so not her thing.

Launching herself up, she darted a glance at Alec. Talk about excellent bed partner. He certainly knew what he was doing. *That's probably because he's slept with every woman from here to Sweden, honey. Don't go thinking it's something it's not.* While she talked her body out of believing all the things Alec had told her last night, she tried to stretch as achy muscles protested in a honey-you-used-muscles-you-had-no-business using way.

Lifting the sheet covering her to the neck, she peeked down. Yeppers, definitely naked. Not at all a dream. As the events of the previous night started to unpeel themselves like an onion, she flushed again. She'd slept with him. More than that, she'd seduced him. And somewhere in the foggy sex haze, she'd asked him to be her date.

Jaya blushed when that memory flooded her brain. Her, kneeling in front of a spectacular erection, refusing to let him come until he promised to do her a huge favor by being her date. The way he coiled his hand in her hair and called her a tease, all the while making his own counter-bargain about seeing her in this position again.

"Oh, God." She cringed when the whisper filled the silence. What had gotten into her last night? She'd barely had anything to drink, so it hadn't been the alcohol clouding her brain. It had been her stupid plans. They'd gotten her jazzed. She'd listened to her friends. Worse, she'd wanted to believe she could be someone different. Once she figured out how to get her life back, her brain had started to think she was invincible—like she could make anything happen. And she had. She peeked under the sheet one more time and still, she wasn't wearing any clothes. Three, no make that four times—with a total stranger. Well at least he hadn't killed her and chopped her up and put her into the freezer. Thank Buddha for little favors.

Okay, must escape before the awkward, gosh-I've-seen-you-naked-now-we-must-make-small-talk conversation. If she could slip out without waking him, she'd never have to see him again. Never mind the fact that she'd asked him to be her date for the wedding. Damn, she'd practically offered to pay him—with her body. She covered her eyes. Moron didn't even begin to cover it.

Okay, girly, find your big-girl panties and bounce. Erm, make that thong. Standing up, she swept from side to side, looking for her dress. Nowhere in the bedroom. A stirring in the bed had her freezing like a cockroach in the daylight. When Alec settled himself back to sleep, she let out a long breath. Right. Dress came off in the living room. She padded out to the main room. Success.

While shoving her arms into the slinky red number, she allowed herself a little pat on the back. Yeah it was a stupid stunt, but God knew she needed it. That was the first time she'd had sex in nine very long months. Since Derrick, actually. She'd gone for it—all out. No holds barred. Problem was, now that she'd had sex-so-good-you-wanna-slap-your-ex, she remembered how much she liked sex—craved it. Even worse, she really liked sex with Alec.

Her body melted into readiness at the mere thought of his sure touch. *Too bad you won't be doing that shit again. Grab your panties and wallet and go.* Except, she still couldn't find her damn panties. They'd been on the table when Alec had taken them off, but she had no idea where they were now. Whatever. She could buy another pair. She grabbed her clutch and made a beeline for the door. Glancing down at her bare feet, she frowned. *Oh, right.* Shoes. She'd kicked them off somewhere around here.

Finding the stupidly expensive shoes under one of the foyer chairs, she slipped them on. Immediately losing her footing, she dropped her purse. *Shit, shit, shit.* Gathering the wayward items, she checked around to see if she could see the panties but couldn't. *Get gone, love.* No more one night stands for you. Most important, no more Alec Danthers. Reckless didn't even begin to cover her behavior. There were reasons for rules. And she was a rule follower to the letter.

FIVE

Alec woke to the scent of roses and a stiff body. He sucked in a deep breath and groaned as his body stirred. *Jaya.* He couldn't help the smile spreading across his face, unable to remember the last time he had sex that actually touched him. *That's because it's been a while, buddy.* Usually, after he met a woman, he forgot her name in minutes, but Jaya's name wasn't one he'd ever forget.

As soon as possible, they needed to do that again. Even while his brain registered the need, his body responded with a surge of lust rushing through his veins, accompanied by the vivid imagery of the previous night. He licked his lips and could still taste her on them—her sweet juices as he circled his tongue around her clit. The way her hands stroked through his hair, then clenched while her body shook in orgasm. The way she'd responded to him, like his every action turned her on, like she'd been made especially for him.

Usually, he couldn't wait to get a woman out of his bed and sight after they had sex. But she wasn't just any woman. And he knew that before he slept with her. A brief flush of regret washed over him when he remembered how hard they'd gone. Once he had a taste of her, there wasn't any going back. What they'd done together would shake him for longer than he cared to think about. Each time he reached for her, she'd been more than willing. She hadn't wanted gentle. The mere thought of her curved form braced against the glass while he smoothed his hands over her ass and up her back as he slid inside her, stroking her g-spot, was enough to bring him to the explosion point. *Damn it.*

The blood pumping through his lap woke the-not-quite-sleeping soldier. Taking his cock in his hand, he meant to just shift him out of the way so he wouldn't wake Jaya, but the moment he touched himself, the urge to stroke was too strong. Wrapping his fingers around the base, he gave a slow, gentle glide down. Then a firmer grip flowing up over the head. Just the way he liked it. "Ahhh." He expelled a long slow breath. Except it wasn't as satisfying as he hoped. He needed more. He needed her.

A good guy would have let Jaya sleep and headed to the bathroom for a nice, icy shower or at least tried for an easy empty release. But that wasn't him. He was a Westhorpe, after all. Men in his family were renowned for their low impulse control. He wanted her. Needed to feel her slick heat around him. Condoms were an unbreakable rule, but Jaya made him wish they didn't need formality. Just the mere thought of her hot heat molding around him as she panted his name made his cock pulse.

Unable to control himself any longer, he reached for her. His arms only pulled in bedding. The sheets on her side of the bed were still warm. Cracking an eyelid open, he was surprised to find that it was already morning, with bright sunlight filtering through the drapery, bathing the suite in gold.

"Jaya? Are you still here?"

No one answered. There was no sound of the shower, no blow dryer, no running water. Just silence.

What the hell? She'd fucked him and then left? Sitting up, he couldn't believe what had happened. Sure, he had more than one one-night stand in his life. Hell, he'd had more than one in the last month. Then why did he feel empty? Throwing back the covers, he did a more thorough scan of the suite. She was definitely gone. *Damn.*

He hadn't even gotten her number. Her real number. Not the bullshit one she gave him on her business card. Right. Because that's what you did with a one-night stand. Called them later. *Dumbass.* He knew better.

He told himself all kinds of lies to make himself feel better. Like if she wanted to use him and bounce, then good for him. The last thing he needed was any kind of entanglement. As soon as he brought back his prodigal brother, he was out of here. Back to Durban. On to the next adventure. Or maybe he needed to put that expedition together to finally make it from the tip of South Africa to the top of Tunisia. That was his ultimate goal.

Maybe it was time to speed up his plans and do something he wanted. With this quick errand for Adele, he didn't need to work for the next year if he didn't want to. That's where his focus should be. Not on some woman he'd seen twice and used up his stash of condoms with. Letting her get under his skin was a mistake. She'd done them both a huge favor by ducking out.

Naked, he strolled into the kitchen following the smell of

the delicious nutmeg coffee. He liked chick coffee, so sue him. Before he could pour the life-giving nectar down his gullet, he slid on something. Frowning, he stared at the two rectangles of plastic at his feet. Bending down to scoop them up, he grinned. She'd left her license and credit card. *Gotcha*.

Maybe it was a little premature to call it game over with Jaya Trudeaux. He tapped the cards against his palm while he waited for his coffee. After all, they owed it to themselves to see if last night was some kind of aberration.

And unlike most women he slept with who left behind souvenirs, he doubted she'd done it on purpose. Given her evasion technique with the business card and that he woke to an empty bed, she was one lady who didn't want to be found.

Well that was just too bad. It was his civic duty to get her belongings back to her. What was a guy to do? Besides, it didn't sit well with him to be left behind. He was the one usually sneaking out of women's apartments in the middle of the night. True, he also never brought anyone back to his place. It was too easy for someone to see part of him he wasn't willing to share.

He completely ignored the burn in his chest every time he thought her name. He wasn't going to look for her because she'd gotten under his skin. Things like that didn't happen to him. She was just a woman. The one woman he'd ever gone after. But it didn't mean anything.

With a renewed zest for the day, he hurried to shower and throw on some clothes. He had a breakfast date to make.

IF THERE WAS a contest for most stupid moments, Jaya counted herself a front runner. She had humiliated herself enough for one seventy-two hour period. Letting herself into her condo, the first thing she did was slip off her stilettos. So much for lucky charms. They were supposed to make her feel sexy and confident. To be fair, they'd done their job, but talk about overconfident. A brief flash of her wearing nothing but the heels as Alec kissed his way up her body warmed her from the inside. After the first time they'd make love, he put them back on for another round.

Damn, she really had to get a control on her hormones. Hot sex? Yes. Great sex? Absolutely. Stupid sex? For sure. What the hell had she been thinking, sleeping with the bartender? So cliché. Her skin still tingled as she remembered the way his lips slid over hers and his tongue probed hers in question and response to hers. The way his hands had yanked her against his hard frame. She'd felt every inch of hard muscle and tasted—

As soon as she remembered the scotch she licked off his body, she felt damp moisture between her thighs—again. Had it been that long since she'd had sex? *Yes.* She hadn't even had a rebound since Mr. I'm-an-asshole-who's-going-to-sleep-with-your-sister. She hadn't even been in the mood for any hanky-panky. The next thing she knew, she was doing the sexy bartender like she'd been trained at the Bunny Ranch in Nevada. Talk about breaking the seal.

Scooping up the gold sparkling shoes, she padded into her bedroom for a shower and change of wardrobe. "Deep breath, Jai. One teeny tiny derailment. You can still get back on course." All she needed to do was find a viable date and come up with a game plan of getting to the client. Brett James mentioned he'd be on vacation for a couple of weeks after they made their decision. So all she needed to do was check to see if Trudeaux got the account. Then Operation Flay-Derrick-I'm-an-asshole-who-slept-with-your-sister was a go. Easy Peasy. Eyes on the prize.

Except as date prospects went, she came up snake eyes. She had no boyfriend, secret or otherwise, no date to the wedding, and no plan yet of what she would say to Brett James if she managed to get him alone. She slid a glance to the clock as she unzipped the Jersey dress. Six-thirty am. Damn, that meant only an hour of sleep before she needed to be up trolling through her contacts. She'd done a lot of favors in her life. Someone could return one. All she needed was someone bright enough to impress her father and drop dead hunky enough to make Tamara salivate. How hard could that be?

A knock at the door had her cursing. Damn Marco. She'd made friends with him in the hopes he'd provide extra security to her first floor condo, but instead, he used their friendship as a reason to stop by at all kinds of crazy hours for chats. Normally she didn't mind as he was hot and Brazilian. But now, she was exhausted. She threw on her favorite pair of UCSD shorts and grabbed the nearest tank top she could find. Screw a bra. She was too tired to deal.

Swinging open the door, she said "Marco, as much as I'd love to chat, I—" Her throat went as dry as the Sahara when instead of Marco, Alec leaned against the doorjamb.

The smile across his lips managed to be sexy and sardonic all at once. "Do you always open the door like that? I could have been an ax murderer or something."

For several moments, Jaya couldn't find her voice. Leave it to her to find the one night stand with some serious detective chops. As far as she was concerned, the possibility of him being an ax murderer wasn't out of the question. At the very least a stalker. When she found her voice, it squeaked. "Did you follow me here? How did you get into the building?" What was the bloody point of paying so much for a doorman building?

He put both hands up. "Relax. I come in peace. Reaching into the inner pocket of his leather jacket he pulled out two small plastic cards. "You left your license and credit card." Tilting his head towards the front door he added, "And, as for Marco, well, turns out he's a sucker for love."

She rolled her eyes, pouring all her acting chops into annoyed nonchalance. Her body, though, traitor that it was, tightened in all sorts of delicious places at the sound of his voice.

"Perfect." Feeling exposed in her tank top and shorts, Jaya wished she'd had the wherewithal to put on something a little less...see-through. But she resisted crossing her arms. If he was offended by her tits, tough. He was in her condo. "Um, thanks for saving me the hassle of chasing them down."

"Alec. You can use my name. Not like you haven't used it before." That annoyingly sexy smile remained. As if he knew just how freaked she was by her behavior last night and wanted to rub it in.

"Thank you, Alec." She cursed the breathy quality of her voice. "But you didn't have to come all the way over here."

His gaze dipped to her chest. "What? You didn't think you could get away with screwing and running, did you? If you hadn't left these behind, I would have asked one of your friends for your number. I've been told I'm charmingly persistent."

Jaya couldn't hear for the blood rushing in her ears. "I— Um." A slow blush crept up her chest to the column of her throat and eventually settled in her cheeks and ears. "Look. I figured I'd save us some awkward small talk and I have a lot of work to do so..." She prayed he'd take the cold-shouldered hint and leave.

So much for prayer.

"How about I take you out for breakfast? I was very disappointed you left without saying goodbye. I mean, no flowers, no jotted-down phone number...you'd think I was a leper."

As he handed over her license, their fingertips brushed. Jaya felt a spark of electricity. Every nerve ending in her body stood at attention, begging, screaming to be touched, fondled, and caressed.

She snatched her hand back.

"We both know you're no leper," she mumbled, even though her brain admonished her mouth for taking the initiative. *Shut up. Shut up.* She really had to stop talking so much. She cleared her throat. What does someone say to a sex-god standing in her doorway? "Right. Anyway. Thank you for the offer of breakfast, but I don't think so. I want to try and get some more sleep and get some work done. I'll let you go enjoy the rest of your night, erm day."

His brow furrowed as he stood erect, shoving his hands in his pockets. "Did I say something wrong?"

"No. I—" She took a breath. "I don't do one-night stands. I'm not that girl. I've never fallen into bed with a perfect stranger. I'm not up on the etiquette, but I'm pretty sure awkward morning-after conversation isn't something the guys look forward to in the a.m., so I blazed. I thought I was doing you a favor."

He quirked a brow. "Oh, come on, Jaya. You ran for *you.* Not for me. You were a little freaked and you bolted. I get it. I've bolted before too. More than once, but we're not going to get into that. The way I figure it, you can come to breakfast with me. Let me charm you a little. I'm only in town for a couple of weeks but—"

"Why me?" She didn't need the whole charm-and-scheme routine. Straight talk worked better.

His face turned serious. "Hands down, you're the sexiest woman I've come across in so long I can't even remember. You're the only woman to get under my skin, and in equal parts it scares the shit out of me and intrigues me."

She narrowed her eyes. "Why should I believe you?"

He shrugged. "Because it's the truth. Because I'm hoping you'll say yes and we can go to breakfast and eventually end up back in bed. And finally, because something besides me is bugging you and I'd like to help if I can."

Rattled by his honesty and sudden perception, Jaya stepped back from him. "Why do you think something's bugging me?"

"For starters, you've crossed your arms over those delicious breasts of yours, which in my book constitutes a crime. Then, you try and give me the brush off even after that jolt of lust.

Yeah I felt it too. And finally, your voice wobbled just the tiniest bit. So either I said something wrong or...." His voice trailed.

Jaya didn't like how well he read her. "You must be a hell of a bartender."

His lips thinned a split second before he spoke. "Amongst other things. You want to tell me what the problem is? I'm told I'm an excellent problem-solver." He shrugged and that easy smile was back to torment her dreams. "Besides, you helped me out tonight, last night, whatever, by getting me out of work. I owe you a flick of my magic wand."

"Unless your magic *wand* is specifically designed to erase the memory of me losing my job three days ago, the fact that my old boyfriend—who, consequently, is the reason I lost my job—is about to marry my sister in two weeks, and also that my father believes I'm a perpetual failure, I doubt there's much you can do."

That sexy, lazy smile widened to a grin. "It turns out I might have just the wand for that."

SIX

ALEC WATCHED WITH BEMUSEMENT AS JAYA'S DELICATELY arched brows shot up. Her eyes darted to his crotch and he bit back a string of curses. "Maybe not the best choice of words." He leaned forward, marveling at the way his body hummed when she swayed toward him.

Before he could talk himself out of being cautious, he cupped her face with his hand, and drew her to him. He knew there were a million reasons why he shouldn't kiss her, shouldn't take her to bed. Too bad he couldn't think of a single one.

His lips slid over hers and he breathed in her scent. The remnants of her perfume made his blood simmer. All he wanted to do was bury himself inside her and shut out the world. When her tongue met his, he felt the jolts of electricity straight to his cock. Groaning against her lips, he pulled her closer to him. She sighed and wound her arms around his neck. As her whole body relaxed, she molded her body against his. Moving his hands to her waist, his thumbs traced a path at the hem of her tank top. She hitched in a breath.

A niggling voice in his head said to wait. His body wanted to shoot that voice. Groaning against her lips, he tried to bring his libido under control. He felt her draw back and lifted his head to look down at her. What the hell was wrong with him? This was not part of the plan.

Jaya squeezed her eyes shut. When they opened again, fatigue had chased off the lust. The words tumbled out of her full lips in a steady flow. "Look, Alec, I'm sorry. I can't. Why did you really come here? What do you want from me? You can't just show up on my doorstep and kiss me and make me forget what I need to do."

He shook his head as he forced his hands into the back pockets of his jeans. "Sorry. I didn't mean to do that."

"It's been a long night and neither one of us got any sleep. I need to start making some calls this morning if I'm going to find a date, and all I want are a couple of hours so I can be coherent. If your ego is bruised because I left this morning, then I'm sorry. It really was the best sex I have ever had in my life. And god-damn, you can kiss. But, it's not you, it's me. I just didn't want to do the awkward thing. Thank you again for bringing back my card and license. I just can't do *this*."

He crossed his arms as he watched her begin to lose steam. "You all done now?"

She didn't look pleased about the interruption but she closed her mouth.

"What I was saying was, I have a solution to your problems."

She put her hands on her hips. "Oh yeah? Somehow I doubt another round of curl-my-toes sex is going to solve my current problems. Now if you'll excuse—"

Alec stepped over the threshold before she could unceremo-niously shut the door in his face. "Okay, relax. Maybe I did come here because my ego was a little bruised, but that's not the only reason. I like you and I really do want to help."

Almond-shaped hazel eyes narrowed at him. "You know anyone who wants to sit through the torture of wedding festivities with my family? I promise you it'll resemble something like ancient torture tests."

"Yeah. Me."

She blinked up at him. Blinked again. The deep breath she choked in drew his attention to her pert breasts. He schooled his brain before the runaway train could go into the memory bank for how sweet they tasted and how her whole body melted every time he licked the dark tips. She opened her mouth to speak then shut it again.

"Wow, cat got your tongue? I'm impressed. Somehow I thought it would take more."

Again, the narrowed eyes, but this time she accompanied them by tossing a tiny stuffed Batman figurine his way. Not bad aim, she almost got him in the head.

"Why would you agree to do something like that? Last night was a one-off. And I know I asked you to be my date, but that was just a sex game. I didn't think you would actually say yes."

Which is really a shame. "Yeah, you said that already. Bottom line is I need something from you too."

She backed up a step. "Is this where you tell me you need a kidney or my beating heart for some whacked ritual?"

He snickered. "You really need to lay off the Law and Order SVU. It's simpler than that. I need an event planner."

"What?"

"Event planner. That is what you do right? I called you the other day. At Trudeaux, they said you didn't work there anymore, which I might mention is not cool, as that's where you wanted me to bill the dry-cleaning. Anyway, I figure you have some time on your hands."

He watched as her shoulders relaxed by degrees. "What kind of event? Something small? At the bar, maybe?"

He shook his head. "Try a thousand—person gala for Adele Westhorpe for the end of the year."

He watched as her mouth did the open-closed guppy thing again, all the while taking in the detail of her place. Everything was hyper-neat and organized. The only thing incongruous was the figurine, and he had a feeling the mini Bruce Wayne didn't spend much time out of place. It was the crack of dawn and her place looked like the maid had just been through it.

"Oh, right, like you know Adele Westhorpe. This sounds like a scam."

That stung. But then, what was she supposed to think? He had been a bartender when he met her. "Yeah, well, my brother isn't the only one who works for the Westhorpes, though my title is a little more ambiguous. I'm sort of the resident Mr. Fix-It. Anything needs dealing with, and I'm the one they call. Last night, they needed bar staff and a general manager for the opening of the club." There. That was almost the truth.

"Why would you give me a job of that magnitude? You don't even know me. I could be a crazy person. Or worse, suck at the event thing."

It was on the tip of his tongue to tell her he knew every inch of her—from what made her smile, to the fact that she talked in her sleep, to what she looked like when she came—but then she probably wouldn't take that well. "I'm not doing you a favor. All I'm getting you is an audition. Adele Westhorpe needs an event planner and she's tasked me with finding her one. It won't be a walk in the park. She's a tyrant. In exchange, I go to this wedding with you."

She swiped a hand across her forehead. "I'm sorry. I'm floored. People don't do this kind of thing for total strangers. I could be a total flake. You're putting your job on the line to help me."

"My mother always did call me impetuous. So is that a yes? Can we go get breakfast now?" His stomach rumbled a second to his request.

"I—wait. I need to be sure. Can we have some kind of contract or something? You know, saying you don't expect sex in return?"

His grin was instant. She drove a hard bargain. "Do you want to tell me why sex isn't on the agenda?"

"You mean, besides muddy waters and I need my total focus on the job at hand? Contrary to my behavior last night, I don't just sleep with random guys. I'm the get-attached girl and clearly you're not a get-attached guy, so it's just easier."

And it won't allow you to have control. But he knew better than to goad her with that tidbit of truth. "Okay, fine. What I will say is this. When you decide you want to sleep with me, it'll have nothing to do with our deal. Can you live with that?"

"You're so sure of yourself."

Why was he pushing so hard? So what if she said no? So what if he never saw her again? He gritted through the pang of loss. It was worse than he thought. Which was why he had to get her out of his system. She wasn't the first woman he wanted or who threatened to become a major distraction for him. He just needed some time to work through it. The added bonus was he could also make Adele happy.

"You'd be surprised, but I've heard that before." He cocked his head. "So, what do you say? Am I date material?"

She eyed him as she worked her bottom lip. It was all he could do to tell her to forget the deal and coax her back to bed.

She let out a long sigh. "Why do I have a feeling I'm going to regret this?"

"I don't know. Why do you?"

"You're too charming for your own good. I'm sure you've heard that before. The way I see it, the charm can either work against me or for me." Jaya pressed a hand to her chest like it was her panacea. "You know I need the job. I just don't know why you're being so nice to me. You don't know me."

He shrugged. "Let's just say, I saw you rock out to old-school Jackson Five, Rihanna and Jason Mrahz. Your musical taste is eclectic and you blow my mind in bed."

She blushed.

"So even if you say it was a one-time thing, and you aren't going to let that happen again, I'm inclined to help you. And you'll be saving my ass. Adele Westhorpe isn't a woman who takes disappointment well. All you have to do is come to breakfast. Then we'll head up to LA."

"LA? That's a two-hour drive. I'm not just going to drop everything I'm doing and go somewhere with you. You could still be an ax-murderer."

"Well, if I were, wouldn't you already be dead by now? And if you worry I'm going to strand you in LA, you can drive."

"Look, this just feels really impulsive and rushed. You don't know me, but I do not do impulsive and rushed. I'm a planner. I'm not heading to Los Angeles on a moment's notice. Besides, what's up there?"

"Adele's in LA. She's interviewing other event planners at

the Westhorpe up there. And let me point out that you've planned out every inch of your life and see where you are now. Maybe it's good to be a little impulsive."

She chewed on her bottom lip and Alec temporarily lost focus. When she sighed, he knew he had her. "Okay. But first I need to send some emails in case this Westhorpe thing doesn't work out. I've got some feelers out there. This condo won't pay for itself."

He grinned. "Now that we're in agreement that I make a wonderful date, can we go eat?"

"Is that all you can think about?"

"You took sex off the table." He shrugged.

Rolling her eyes, she hitched up her shorts again, hiding the strip of flesh under the cotton fabric. "Okay. Fine. I figure we need to—" The jangling of keys in the lock had her head whipping around. Using her whole body to barricade the door, she whispered, "This will sound crazy, but—"

"You need me to hide in the bathroom, closet, or bedroom?"

Her eyes bugged. "How did you know?"

He shook his head. "I've had enough encounters that ended this way while someone had to explain to a boyfriend, or husband or lesbian lover."

She giggled as she slapped a hand over her eyes. "Incorrigible. But somehow I believe it."

He grinned. "I'll just make myself comfy in your bedroom."

"Thank you." She nodded in the direction of the hallway and he reluctantly complied.

"Okay, but I will ask some questions later."

She shoved her full weight behind the door again. Whoever was on the other side couldn't have been much bigger than she was, as he or she couldn't budge her from the door frame. "I promise you, it's not a husband or anything. Just something too awkward to explain and deal with. Please." she whispered.

He sauntered down the hallway, straining to hear. He opted to stop in the bathroom. It was closer and would probably afford a better eavesdropping spot. And to think, he almost walked away from all this intrigue.

SEVEN

Jaya braced herself against the door once more. Could she really do this? Have this show down with Tamara when she knew Alec was down the hall eavesdropping? Tams was the only other person who had a key. Another hard knock resounded through the wood. Whether she wanted to have the conversation or not, Tamara was coming in.

"Jai, it's Tamara. I need to speak with you." For a second, Jaya considered climbing out the window, but she'd never been that much of a coward. Drawing in a deep breath, she muttered to herself, "You can do this." She stepped back, allowing Tamara in.

Her sister stumbled in, carrying a medium sized box. "Damn it, you need to get your door fixed. I know it's summer, but there's no excuse for a swollen door in a building like this. It's not like you are in some really old prewar building or something."

As usual, accompanying Tamara was an air of disorganization and chaos. Jaya reigned in her already crackling temper.

What the hell was her sister doing here? Here, when she had Alec in her apartment. She didn't need Tamara reporting back to her father how Jaya had some one night-stand staying at her place. "What are you doing here, Tamara? I've got a busy day." Her eyes made an involuntary dart towards the hallway. What was he doing in her bedroom? Before her imagination could gallop off with that thought, she focused on her sister. "It's early."

Tamara barged past her. "Sometimes, I swear you think I'm your enemy."

"Come on in, why don't you," Jaya muttered under her breath, refusing to feel the twinge of guilt. Tamara had already proven she didn't care about her feelings.

Placing the box she carried on the couch, she turned to face Jaya. "You left this at the office. It's your personal stuff. Derrick had me clean it out for you. I offered to bring it by instead of sending a courier."

As Tamara scrutinized her, Jaya shifted under the gaze. "Thanks. You shouldn't have bothered." If everything went the way she hoped, she'd have to cart it right back to the office anyway.

Tamara's gaze shifted from Jaya's. "I wish you'd said something before you left the office. I was really gutted when Derrick told me. I never thought he'd go through with something like that." Tamara shifted from one foot to another. "I mean, I know you two have your differences and everything. If you want, maybe I can talk to Dad and—"

Jaya's brows drew up. "Exactly what would you say in my defense? 'Geez, honey, go easy on my sister—we owe her after all?'"

Tamara ignored the jibe. "Well, you probably didn't need to

disobey Dad and do that specific presentation. You could have done the one Dad and Derrick approved."

Weary, Jaya rolled her shoulders. She didn't need to rehash her greatest failure over and over again. Especially not with Alec in ear-shot. But she couldn't let it go. "In the office, I was an equal employee. It was my account and my client, so I had the right to give the pitch any way I wanted. And it got us the client's business, if today's newspaper is correct." Jaya could hear the tone of her voice and the increasing decibels, so she forced her breathing into an even cadence. "You're not here to talk about how I got fired, so what do you need?"

Tamara shifted again in her Prada loafers and adjusted her purse strap. "I, um, wanted to see if you'd still be at the wedding."

Jaya cocked her head. "Tamara, I—"

Tamara held up a hand. "Look, I know you hate me. You have every right to feel that way and to not come, but I'd hoped maybe you'd still be willing to support me. Since Mom's not here, you know. You're the only one I have close to a mother and—"

There it was. The familiar guilt. Because, even though she was younger, Jaya had always been the one to take care of her sister. There'd been a point when they were inseparable. Right before Tamara swiped Derrick out from under her nose. But Tamara was still her sister. "I don't hate you." *Just your leech of a fiancé.* "I told you I'd be there. I'm not happy about it. I wish I could be happy for you, but considering the circumstances, I'm not that altruistic." She sucked in a breath, because that was what you did for family. "But you're my sister. I'll be there."

Tamara nodded her thanks, knowing better than to offer a hug. Jaya had tried for almost a year to let go of some of the anger. After all, it wasn't as if she still wanted Derrick. He was an asshole. But the betrayal of her sister still didn't sit well. And her father's acceptance of it all, as if nothing had ever happened, bit the big hairy one. But she was an adult. She could get over it—well, mostly. This was her sister and family was everything. She'd promised her mother.

"Oh." Tamara turned on her heel. "Are you sure you won't be bringing a date?"

Jaya opened her mouth to say she wasn't sure--after all, nothing was set in stone until Adele Westhorpe said yes to hiring her. But before she could answer, Alec and his sexy shoulders ambled through her bathroom door with a grin.

"Yep, she'll have a date." He thrust out a strong hand. "Alec Danthers, nice to meet you."

Tamara's jaw hung open as she did the stare-and-ogle thing up at Alec. Not like Jaya could blame her. She knew how beautiful he was to look at from all angles. Her sister's jaw was flapping so hard, she only managed a soft stutter. "T-Tamara."

There was no shock in his face as he looked back and forth between the two of them. They looked enough alike that most people assumed they were twins. Only someone paying close attention would know they weren't.

"You must be Jaya's sister. I've heard a lot about you."

It took several attempts, but Tamara finally found her voice. "I—we—um." she cleared her throat. "Jaya hasn't said anything about you."

He nodded in understanding, making Jaya want to slap him. "Well you know your sister. Keeps things close to the chest. Jaya wanted to keep me quiet for a bit."

As Jaya watched their exchange in disbelief, she had a hard time working her vocal cords. She wanted to clock Alec with something, shove her sister out the door, and burn the box of her office things, but somehow that didn't fit in with the behavior of a full-grown adult, so all she said was, "Um, yes, been keeping Alec under wraps."

Alec continued. "We're actually heading up to LA today if you want to join us. I'd love to get to know Jaya better through you."

Tamara blinked, as if she couldn't fathom the god talking to her again. "N-nice of you to offer, but I have wedding planning." She glanced back at her sister and mouthed "Wow," then stumbled on unsteady feet toward the front door. "I'll check in later, okay?"

She turned with a scowl to Alec. "Well, I guess you answered for me."

He grinned back at her. "I guess I did."

IT WASN'T LIKE he kidnapped her. Okay. Maybe a little like he kidnapped her. At the very least, he coerced her with a heavy hand. But he needed her if he wanted to be on his way in two weeks. *Ends and means, Alec. Ends and means.* He slid a glance in her direction. Her lithe frame lounged against the door frame of the Lotus. "You know, I'm not so bad."

She rolled her eyes at him. "Says the man who manipulated me into coming to Los Angeles with him."

A grin spread across his face. He liked spunky. "Oh, come on. It'll be fun. You know I'm a good time." He winked.

"And incorrigible," She said with a laugh. Shaking her head, she added. "Do you do things like this all the time? Just take off?"

"Sure. Drives you nuts, huh?"

"You might not have things to do, but I do. What if your supposed lead doesn't pan out? Then I wasted a perfectly good day going off the plan."

He navigated around the suburban going sixty in the fast lane. "Did you just say 'off plan'? Can't plan out your whole life, sweetheart. Just doesn't work that way."

"Says the Jack-of-All-Trades for the Westhorpe family." She sat up straighter in her seat. "How do you expect to do anything without a plan?"

"Tell me, Jai, do your plans ever leave time for any fun? You seem uptight."

"I'm not uptight." She said as she sat up prim and stiff in her seat. "I'm practical. You strong-armed me into coming with you. Why couldn't you just ask me out like a normal guy?"

He barked out a laugh. "You think this is because I want—"

The piercing tone of an incoming call broke off his thought. The caller ID said Mimi. His mother always had impeccable timing. He opted for the Bluetooth in his ear, in case she was in one of her moods. His mother could be difficult. But you didn't choose your family. Especially when they took you in.

"Mimi, how are you?"

"Don't use that smooth-talker tone with me. I know you. Hell, I raised you. It didn't work then, and it's not working now."

"I can't help that I'm naturally charming."

"Sometimes you act like you're your father's son. But I know better."

Ouch. He sucked in a breath, casting Jaya a glance out of the corner of his eye. She studiously ignored him. "What can I do for you?"

"Are you on your way up here? I want to debrief on where we are with the Maxwell situation."

"I'm heading there now. I've got a lead I want to follow up. I'll debrief you afterward."

"Are you going to tell him why you're looking for him? I suggest—"

"I got it." He interrupted. "I'll deal with him and will let you know. It'll be fine. He'll be safe and sound at home in no time. Trust me." As usual, his mother would try and control the situation. But this time she needed to let him handle things.

Ever since he showed up on the doorstep and declared Royce Westhorpe his father, Adele had taken him in. She'd read his father the riot act when he'd wanted to throw the scrawny boy out on his ass. After his birth mother died, he'd taken the only things he had of value, his birth certificate and letters from Royce to his mother that were a decade old. He'd taken a cab and two buses from El Cajon, determined to find his father before CPS could toss his ass into the system.

The old man had called security to cart his ass out, but Adele stood firm. After some blood work and attempts to find other family members, plus a quick call to social services, she'd had him tucked into the Westhorpe's elaborate mansion. At the time she didn't have any children, so she'd been in full mother-lion protective mode. While the tests were running, she'd given him a place to stay and looked out for him, kept Royce away from him, keeping him safe until the truth could be determined. She'd never wavered that he should be looked after. And when the happy news had arrived that he was, in fact, a Westhorpe, she'd declared he was living with them instead of at boarding school, like Royce suggested.

Even after Max had arrived, she still treated him like her own. Groomed him, educated him, and loved him.

"Don't sound so flippant, Alec. This isn't one of those situations where you can reason with Max to come home. He's in a world of trouble if you can't find and contain him."

As she scolded him, he wondered when she'd started to sound so weary. An invisible fist squeezed his heart. He needed to keep her calm and in decent, if not necessarily good, spirits.

"Mimi, have I ever let you down?"

She sighed. "No, but—"

"I won't let you down now, either. You can count on me. So, relax. I'll call you when we get in."

She may have been old and ill, but she was still as sharp as ever. "We?"

"That's right. I'm bringing you a present."

EIGHT

THIS WAS WHAT HAPPENED WHEN JAYA DIDN'T FOLLOW script. She ended up in the poshest waiting area she'd ever seen, with its sleek, outrageously expensive, contemporary furniture, staring up at a photo of dragon lady, vying for the job of her life. Not to mention, she was sitting next to a man she barely knew who'd given her the best sex of her life. Jaya shifted uncomfortably in the low backed, white leather waiting room seat and tried not to show her nerves—pretty hard to pull off, since her knees were doing their MC Hammer impression. She needed this job. So far, it was her only lead in case operation get-Daddy-to-rehire-her didn't work as expected.

The rail-thin receptionist gave her a wan smile. "You may go in now. Ms. Westhorpe only has ten minutes to spare."

Geez. How the hell was she supposed to impress in only ten minutes? Somehow she doubted her geek super-status would qualify her as hire-worthy.

Alec's strong hand on her knee made her jump.

"Go on in. Adele doesn't bite. I promise."

She might not bite, but Jaya had a feeling she barked really loud.

"Yeah, sure. Fine."

"I told you. She'll love you. Just go on in and be—" Alec's gaze flicked over her prim and proper suit and killer $3,000 stilettos, "you. Just be you. I'll meet you in the lobby around three. We'll tour the hotel afterwards."

Jaya should have been focusing on what he was saying. Instead, she was too busy eyeing the male figure leaving Adele Westhorpe's office. He looked ill. His eyes said, "Give me a moment to clear" and his posture said, "I've just been whipped with a shoe." His knuckles were white with a side of Casper.

Her feet rooted into the floor. Going in there didn't seem like an option. But really, what choice did she have? It was either this or go to Tamara and Derrick's wedding sans date.

But if there was one thing Jaya was good at, she could fake it 'til she made it. That was a skill she'd mastered early. Striding into the office, she closed the door behind her. "Ms. Westhorpe, I'm Ja—"

The older woman cut her off. "I know who you are. If I wanted introductions, I'd have invited you to a garden party. "

Whipcord-lean, Adele Westhorpe looked fit for a woman her age. Shit, for a woman any age. Jaya had a feeling the woman never indulged in cookies and cream, the likes of which made Jaya afraid to look at her scale.

As she sat across from the Westhorpe matriarch, all Jaya could think of was how the woman could give the devil a run for her money. *If you don't nail this interview, your failure status will be solidified.* If she made it through this interview, she wouldn't be dateless to her sister's wedding. She'd be elevated from desperate loser status. At least, for a little while. Not to mention, the Westhorpes were just the kind of client Trudeaux would love on their roster. Fail at this and, well—she didn't want to think what would happen if she failed.

She cleared her throat. "Fair enough, ma'am. You know why I'm here. How about you tell me what you're looking to do for the end-of-year anniversary gala, and I'll tell you what I can provide." She helped herself to a seat on the soft chaise instead of in the uncomfortable monstrosity across from the scary woman.

The old lady pursed her lips. Her salt-and-pepper hair, cut in a sleek Anna Wintour bob, framed her face. It should have looked severe, but it somehow made her prettier. If pretty was a word you used to describe a dragon. And now Jaya had poked her with a stick. *Just perfect.*

Looking from Jaya to the chair across her desk, the old bat's lips turn up at the corners, but she remained silent. Jaya usually tried to hold out for a client to speak, but she had a feeling Adele Westhorpe could out wait the devil.

She busted out her notes. "What sort of theme are you looking for?"

Adele gave a slight nod, as if she approved Jaya's jumping right into business.

"Dancing on the Eiffel Tower in the evening."

Wow. As descriptions went, Jaya usually had more vague clients and she had to pull teeth just to get a response. Not Adele, though. She knew what she wanted. "Do you want candle light, or do you have a preference for LED?"

Adele pursed her lips again. Not good. Pursed lips were never a good sign. "They might be green, but they look tacky."

Tacky. Check. No to tacky. Jaya nodded. "Done. Food?" She clicked her pen in nervous habit.

Adele waved a hand. "I'm tired of the same old boring benefit food. Even when it's expensive, it still tastes like rubber and it's never enough. I want something exotic, but light. Nothing too heavy or so unrecognizable the plebeians won't eat it."

Yikes. Plebeians. She cleared her throat. "Music? I'm thinking given the Paris theme, a big, jazzy band." Another pursed lip. So far not so great. *Get it together, Trudeaux.* No assumptions with this woman.

"You'd be wrong. I might look old and moneyed, but I want this to be a party. So there has to be dancing. And not that boring, old-people stuffy shit. I want lively dancing. Though I really do hope to refrain from that Britney Spears type of poppy fluff."

Jaya fiddled with her pen, rolling it between her fingers. Her pinky's gray polish gleamed as the light hit it. She wasn't sure what warranted the most surprise, that Adele Westhorpe had just said shit or that she knew who Britney Spears was. "Okay, how about Nina Simone? She's classic, and her up-tempo songs can play in the background. Mix in a little Joe Cocker, James Brown and Billie Holiday."

Adele nodded. Her finger tapping her chin. "Yes, I do enjoy Nina. But I want something youthful, too. That Beyoncé girl. She's good. Make sure there's some of her."

Well, well. Who knew Beyoncé's music would have filtered into a billionaire's sphere of knowledge? Jaya took notes for the next seven minutes. Adele made commentary on everything from the dress to the decor. Flashy but not gaudy. A hint of the holiday season as a nod to the timing, but no over-the-top decorations. The guest list would come later, but the members of the board would be there and the employees not working that night would also be invited. All those who had to work would be thrown a different party. Jaya took notes like she already had the job. No sense trying to redo the info-gathering.

Jaya wrote at all kinds of break-neck speeds until she realized Adele was no longer speaking. She looked up from her notepad into the expectant face of the Westhorpe owner. *Shit. Now or never. Do your pitch, girlie, and get it right.*

"The feeling, as we discussed, is dancing at the top of the Eiffel Tower. So the theme will be lights of Paris. We'll use candles where we can. Those floating ones would be great if we can get a water feature. Also, hanging ones just above the guests' heads. We'll do holly and mistletoe as a nod to the holidays but otherwise, we'll downplay the season. Music choices, we'll hire a band." She put up a hand to stop Adele's impending protest. "One young enough that they know how to play Beyoncé and Katy Perry, but with big band capabilities to do real justice to Nina, James and Billie."

She took a quick breath and plowed on. No reason to give Adele a chance to say no before she was done. "As for the food, I suggest Gael's Fusion in La Jolla. They do a lovely round-the-world sampling that will have your guests trying Kenyan stew, along with Indian curry and Scottish mutton. He does a lovely small-sized sampling."

Before Adele could remind her that she didn't want appetizers or those boring hors d'oeuvres, Jaya barreled on. "Of course I'll have him do a sampling for you, so you can see the portion sizes. He'll modify to your tastes. And finally, the venue." She drew in a breath. "While it is technically a Westhorpe party, might I suggest a different locale? The gallery space in downtown San Diego on Kettner. It's not the usual posh and swank that your guests are accustomed to, but it will give you the industrial feel of being on the Eiffel Tower. And the penthouse loft has garage doors as windows that we can slide up to give a spectacular view of San Diego.

"We'll use invisible rails for safety, of course, since there will be alcohol."

Jaya finished talking and drew in a breath. Had she gotten it right? She forced her body into calm as she straightened her back. Adele would either love it or hate it. Nothing she could do about it now. She'd given it her best. When her quarry said nothing, but went back to the papers on her desk, Jaya wasn't sure if she should speak or not.

Was that it? Was she just dismissed as if she'd never been there? *Holy rudeness.* She stood abruptly. A small tearing sound had her looking down at her jacket. Nothing. She smoothed down her black tailored pants and found the source of the ripping—the seam in the back. Perfect end to the interview from hell.

Using her portfolio cover, she covered her butt and strode to the door. Jaya didn't need Adele knowing about her wardrobe malfunction. Put-together event planners didn't have these kinds of things happen to them. She'd be dammed if she let this woman make her feel like her father had.

In an even tone, she said, "I'll anticipate your answer by the end of the week." Then she stalked to the door. But not before hearing another tearing sound from the back of her pants. Three days with Cookies and Cream would do that to a Stella McCartney suit. *Shit.* Could this week get any worse? Whatever. She'd given it her best shot. Maybe she could still convince Alec to do the date thing? He asked her to try with no guarantees. So what if—

"You've got spunk."

Jaya used her purse to cover her behind as she whipped around to face the older woman. Maybe she'd stepped in it, but so be it. She wasn't going to run around and kiss anybody's ass. She needed a job and she'd given a strong pitch, considering she had nothing to go on and an hour to get ready. "I've heard that before. Most people call it nerve."

Adele actually smiled. A genuine warm smile and it transformed her face. Jaya could only stare as her eyes softened and smile lines appeared. "I like nerve. Are you sure you can work for me? I don't tolerate fools and I hate stupidity which can make me difficult. You don't seem like a fool or an idiot, so maybe we'll get along."

Was that a job offer? Jaya couldn't tell. Even as she opened her mouth, she knew she should shut it. But then, she'd always had trouble controlling her words. "Well, I don't do bullies and tyrants. The jury's still out on you."

This time, Adele laughed. A genuine belly laugh and Jaya staggered back, unsure what to do. Adele reached out a hand. "Leave your portfolio. I'll get it back to you. And yes, you'll know by early next week." She shook her head as she scanned Jaya up and down. "You know, I didn't think Alec would ever make it happen. But he continues to surprise me."

Cocking her head, she asked, "But wasn't it his job to find you an event planner?"

After taking Jaya's portfolio, she sat back down with a beatific smile. "That's not what I'm talking about, love."

ALEC KNEW he was on a fool's errand. He also knew it probably wasn't a good idea to leave Jaya alone with Adele. But he couldn't be in two places at once. Besides, what's the worst that could happen? From the workup Caleb had pulled on Jaya, he knew she had a good idea what she was doing. And that was the most important thing with Adele. She didn't suffer fools. But Jaya was smart and capable and loved to plan.

"It's a match made in heaven," he muttered to himself. "Stop worrying and focus on getting Max back so you can get back to your life."

He pulled up to the swank, modern two-story bungalow nestled in the hills of Mulholland Drive. This part of the road was littered with windy, twisty alleyways and make-your-knees-hurt hills. But the properties were gorgeous and Max's place was no different. He had to smirk at the bungalow's defiant nod to the sixties as the properties surrounding it had been modernized to reflect sleek modern architecture.

Glancing up at the house, he searched the windows, but couldn't see anything. "What the hell did you expect, moron? Max in the front window holding out a drink for you?" He shook his head. His brother may make bad decisions, but at the end of the day, he wasn't stupid. The only reason Alec even knew about the property was because of Max's obsession with Patsy Klein. She'd supposedly lived in this house when it was first built. Max had paid cash for it years ago under a corporation name.

Leaving the car unlocked, he strode toward the front door, opting for the brash route. It's not like Max didn't know why he was there. And it's not like his brother didn't have some pride. He wouldn't run. He'd refuse to come home, but he wouldn't run.

A clang came from the back door area and he wondered if his little brother had guests. Jogging around the back, Alec used the code to open the back fence. This may be one of the coolest places in the Hollywood hills, but their father had been a stickler for security and instilled that one hard rule: Protect yourself. There was no point in leaving yourself open to disaster. Too bad Max used the same password for everything.

Swinging in the gate, Alec found his brother lying out on a lounge chair with a whole lot of "what the fuck" plastered on his face. Sloshing his drink, he jerked upright. "Alec, what the hell are you doing here?"

"Chasing your ass all over God's green. What do you think I'm doing here? Adele couldn't find you. You haven't been picking up your phone. And every time she sends someone after you, all your properties are buttoned up like Victorian hookers."

Max stood, open shirt sleeves flapping in the breeze. He darted a furtive glance around. "How did you find me? Did you come alone? Is Mom out front?"

Alec had to shake his head. They might be as far apart as the mountains of the Grand Canyon in temperament, but they were near carbon copies of each other when it came to their looks. Their jaws, their eyes, the Roman noses. No one wouldn't mistake them for brothers. Except Alec's dark hair favored his mother and Max's.

Lucky for you, I don't think Adele knows about this place. Otherwise she might have sent her security. She's pissed."

Max grabbed at the hair on his head with his left hand. "Of course you would know where to come find me. You didn't tell her where I was, did you?"

"No. I'll let you keep your sanctuary, but you've got to come home, bro. This mess you're in, it won't clean itself up. And—" he sucked a breath in past the emotion, "—Adele is torn up."

Max's eyes narrowed. "Don't you worry about mom. I'm

sure she's just as tough as she ever was." He sagged a little, letting the bitter edge to his tone seep out. "Look. I know I'm in a world of trouble. I just needed a couple of days to sort myself out. I'm going to go back."

Alec shoved his hands in his pockets, needing to channel the urge to hit his brother into somewhere less destructive. "What the hell were you thinking? Adele wanted me to look into why the Westhorpes with clubs are losing cash. I've had a quick look at the accounts. I assume it's gambling? The Sandovals are the only ones you can get into that much debt with around San Diego. Have you lost your fucking mind? Why the hell didn't you call me?"

"And say what? 'Dude, I fucked up bad.' You would have told me to handle my shit."

That did sound like him. "You know better than that. If I'd known it was this bad, I would have helped you."

Max rolled his eyes and some of the amber liquid in his glass sloshed. "That's right. St. Alec, to the rescue. I can't go back."

The hairs on Alec's neck stood up. "You don't really have a choice. This is some serious shit. Imagine what this is doing to Sue."

Disbelief contorted Max's face. "Don't you talk about Sue. You don't know anything about her."

"You're right. I don't. Other than the fact that she's pregnant. I know nothing about your life or hers. But I do know the real reason you booked like Michael Johnson in oh-eight. You're a selfish asshole. Dude, you left your pregnant fiancée behind after you drained your trust fund. Who does that?"

Max's jaw tightened. "Adele sent you to keep things quiet. She doesn't want anyone at Westhorpe knowing what a screwup her son is."

"Thing is, little brother, you only owed three hundred. I had Caleb check. Why did you drain your trust fund? What kind of trouble are you really in? Even you aren't callous enough to leave Sue behind without any money."

"Look. I know what you think, but it's bigger than just the money I took. I'm going to come back. Just not now. I need more time to figure it out."

"What the hell are you talking about? You can be a selfish little prick, but you're not a complete bastard."

Max's grin went from surly to evil. "Nope, that's your job title, right? Westhorpe Bastard. Has a nice ring to it, doesn't it."

Alec tried to reason with his mind and emotions, telling himself that they were just words. That Max didn't really believe what he was saying. That he wasn't just an errand boy, that he really couldn't hurt his brother. But his fists didn't feel like listening as they clenched and unclenched at his sides. "Enough screwing around, Max. Get your scrawny ass in the car. I'm taking you back."

"Or what, you'll drag me kicking and screaming?"

Alec leveled a glare at his brother. He was spoiling for a fight. "If it comes to that."

Then Max did the unexpected—the one thing Alec was completely unprepared for. He ran.

NINE

ALEC WAS LATE. BUT THEN, JAYA EXPECTED NOTHING LESS. Prompt time wouldn't be on Mr. Fast and Loose's radar. It would be the proper end to the day she'd had. She checked the time again on her phone. Thirty minutes late. Maybe Alec *had* abandoned her in Los Angeles. She should have just driven herself. Or better yet, not come at all. She felt like she could be in a MasterCard commercial. Drive to Los Angeles, two hours. Waiting room time, ten minutes. Time spent humiliating oneself by splitting pants in front of Adele Westhorpe, then subsequent hour trying to find needle and thread, priceless. It's wasn't even like her pitch to Adele had been successful. She'd pretty much blown it with her big mouth. She usually aimed for capable and organized, but this time she'd come across as a pain in the ass with too much to say. When Alec said make an impression, pretty sure being a klutz wasn't the impression she was been going for.

Letting her obsessive personality come out to play, Jaya checked her phone again. Three more minutes. How much longer could she wait there without acting? If she wanted to get back to San Diego tonight, she'd need a cab to the train station. "Okay, ten more minutes, Jai. Then I'm outta here. No sitting around waiting for a man to rescue you," she mumbled to no one in particular. The hotel bar was blissfully empty. No one questioned her when she'd spilled a couple of tears after the interview with Dragon Lady.

Scooting up to the bar, she pulled out her laptop again. If she had to wait, she might as well prep a proper pitch. Not like she expected Adele to offer her a gig, but as exercises went, it would keep her mind off the jobless situation. It was what she loved, thrived on. She was meant to do a job like this.

She had to thank Alec for at least giving her the chance. He didn't know her, but he already felt like a knight in shining armor. If she believed in such things. Rolling her shoulders, she told herself to relax. He would come. She would have something to eat, try to enjoy her meal, and forget about the interview. And maybe even try to not obsess that not one single person had called her back about a job yet.

She might have screwed up in front of Adele, but as far as the rest of the city was concerned, she was a darned good event planner and—

The smell of sandalwood and something else woodsy enveloped her.

"I'm sorry I'm late. Something came up." Directly behind her, Alec's smooth baritone cradled her like a blanket and she almost forgot how her morning went.

She swiveled on the bar stool to face him and choked out a strangled cry. "Oh my God, what happened to you?" As she stood to inspect one of his bruises, she upended her purse. "Damn it." He helped her as she frantically tried to grab the pieces of her life from skittering away. Jaya breathed a sigh of relief as her fingers fell on her Thirty list. Not exactly the kind of thing she wanted floating around. The list may not have her name on it, but the thought of anyone ever reading it made her nauseated. She was so relieved she got a hold of it before Alec could see it. Mortified wouldn't even begin to cover it if he saw what was on there.

He frowned as he glanced down his ragged shirt and dirt-streaked jeans. "I suppose I look a little worse for wear."

She grimaced. "Worse for wear? You look like you've been in an alley fight. And did you know you have a leaf stuck in your hair?"

He grasped for it. "What? Still? I thought I got the last one in the car. Guess not."

All she could do was blink at him for several moments. Then laugh at the absurdity. "What did you do to yourself?"

Sounding like he was trying to hold back a strangled laugh, he said, "You mean besides traipsing through the jungles of LA? Not too much. How did it go with Adele?"

"Erm, great," she lied. No point in hashing out the tortured details right away. He'd find out soon enough. No need for him to know she blew it. "You know—I did a pitch, she heard me out. I guess we'll see." She shrugged, each word leaving a bitter tasting paste in her mouth.

He studied her, the smudge of dirt on his nose the only thing she could see. "Don't take it too hard. Adele's—tough. I'm sure you did all right."

Yeah. Right. If all right meant she'd be eating Top Ramen for the rest of her life just to pay her mortgage. Or worse, have to move back home. She shook her head to clear it. "I'm not going to think about it now. I've got some other things in the hopper, so we'll see."

He nodded, a dark curl flopping on his brow. "Well, a deal's a deal. You came up here, you made the pitch. So I'm your man for this wedding shindig. What do I need to know? I met the evil sister. You know you two could be twins, which, by the way, is very hot." He flashed a grin. "Anyone else? When do I meet the evil ex-fiancé-slash-sister's-new-fiancé?"

She stared at him, not sure what was funnier, that he'd used the word shindig or that he was covered in dirt and debris yet acting as if everything was completely normal. She let out a strangled giggle. "Look, I'm sorry, but you can't just come in here like nothing's off. You're covered in dirt and look like you did the Bachata with a dumpster. Luckily, you don't smell like it." No, he smelled like sandalwood and heaven and she had to fight not to think about the previous night. *No hanky-panky.* That was her rule not his. *Why did I make the stupid rule again?*

"Bachata huh? You ever been to the birthplace of Bachata?" He smiled, and the corners of his eyes creased. "Man, they do know how to party in the Dominican."

She shook her head. "No. Closest I've been is Haiti, to help with the relief efforts. It's where my family originated from generations ago. Most of them eventually ended up in New Orleans."

He swiped at the sweat on his nose then frowned as the dirt came on his finger. "Damn. I'm a mess. I promise I don't take women out looking like this. If Adele saw me, she'd freak." He stood and held out a hand. "Come on. Let me show you around."

She darted a glance around. "Aren't you going to get cleaned up?"

The rakish grin was back complete with dazzling teeth. "That's where we're going." Before she could remind him of their arrangement, he held up his hands in a gesture of peace. "Relax, Jai, I remember the deal. No funny business." He made a cross over his heart. "Scout's honor."

"Were you ever a Boy Scout?"

He chuckled. "Something like that."

She placed her palm in his, noticing the knuckles were raw and pink. Tugging on his hand, she looked up at him. "Please tell me what happened today. Adele Westhorpe doesn't have you doing anything dangerous, does she? Like with teamsters or anything?" She'd seen that in a movie once.

He blinked at her, once, twice, then again. The bellowing laughter that spilled out from him filled her with a rush of instant warmth.

"Adele. Teamsters." Laying a hand on his flat stomach, he guffawed again. "That's awesome. I really must tell her one day."

Jaya frowned. "Maybe not before she has a chance to decide about the job, okay?"

Still chuckling, he shook his head. "No. No teamsters. But the guy I was supposed to bring back to the office had other plans and ran down an alley. I went after him to try and, um, talk to him, but he threw a fist or two, then tossed a dumpster in my path." Wiggling the fingers on his left hand, he gave her a wry smile. "Hence the pink knuckles. I'm fine, really. When are you going to tell me about your wedding?"

"You really *did* do the Bachata with a dumpster."

He leaned in so close she could smell the mint on his breath. "If you like, I can show you how it's done sometime."

The hint of teasing and familiarity sent a sizzle to her core. She cleared her throat. "Maybe it's something I'll add to my Thirty list."

He pulled her through the lobby toward the elevator. As they went, several hotel guest and staff stared, but no one questioned or made attempts to stop them. "What the heck is a Thirty list?"

She followed him into the elevator, a hot flush spread over her skin and she prayed he didn't notice. "Just a list of all the things I want to do before I hit thirty."

He grinned. "Like a Bucket List. I'm glad to hear I made it."

She rolled her eyes. He was just so cocky. "Not you. Sad to say, 'make love to hot stranger in a random hotel' did not make my list. But learning Bachata will. As will dancing on top of the Eiffel Tower in an evening gown."

"You think I'm hot?"

She smacked him on the arm as the elevator dinged on the pool level. "You really can't help yourself, can you?"

"Nope." His grin clearly stated his unabashed delight in himself. "So, can I see it?"

"Oh, hell no." No one saw her list. Not even Micha and Ricca. They were her private goals. She was the only one who saw it and when she crossed things off.

"Wait, you'll tell me what's on it, but you won't let me see it?"

"I only told you two things. It's private. Like, really private. I don't show it to anyone." Lest they judge her by her failures. Like the time she'd tried to ride the New York City subway all night, just to get a vibe of the city. Big mistake. She'd been mugged. He didn't need to know that. Her whole life, she had two mottos. Never let them see you sweat, and never let them see you fail.

"Let me guess. It's one of your rules."

She crossed her arms. "I like my rules." But her conviction

didn't sound as solid as it would have two days ago. After all, sleeping with a stranger was a no-no in her book. Was Micha right? Was she too uptight with too many restrictions? The tiny voice in her head argued. *But if you didn't have your rules, how would you live?* Everything would be in chaos. And she hated disorder. *No, you don't. It's your father who hates chaos. You want to be free.* She shook her head and ignored the voice. She *needed* her list of dos and don'ts. But as she watched Alec out of the corner of her eye, she wondered if she could relax some of her rules.

The muscles in his forearms quivered as he pushed up his sleeves. "Cat got your tongue?"

"No." She flushed and looked down at her hands. "I've been meaning to say, thank you. This job, if it pans out, is something I needed. I'm not sure what I did right. But thank you."

He remained silent. She brought her eyes up to meet his. And he smiled. "You don't have to thank me. Believe me you're doing me a favor."

"And the wedding? Is that doing you a favor too?"

"Oh yes." He winked.

"How exactly?" "

"I get to spend the next two weeks with a beautiful, sexy woman."

She flushed. "You shouldn't flirt with me like that."

"What if I like flirting with you? What if I like making you flush pink under that pretty brown skin?"

She didn't exactly know what to say to that. So she played with the hem of her shirt and changed the subject to something safer. "I sent out a ton of query letters to event planning companies around town, looking for a bite or referral. They all know my work. They were competitors and pseudo friends. All of a sudden, my email is either being ignored or they're not getting back to me. One actually replied that he knew my father well and if I'd left, it must be for a reason." She sniffed in an effort to keep the waterworks at bay.

A frown line marred his otherwise smooth forehead. "Word got around quick, huh?"

She gnawed on her lower lip. "Well, seeing how it's a Saturday and I left on Tuesday, the only way for word to have gotten out is if someone spread it. Which is possible. Or it's something else."

"Something else like...?"

"Like Dad is deliberately blocking my chances to get another job."

"But why would he do that? What's your story with him anyway? Why would he stand in your way?"

"My father and I—our relationship is tense. I'm the least like him, so I try harder to please him. He's austere and doesn't show his emotion unless it's with Tamara. He actually smiles at her. With me, all he sees is 'not good enough.' Even if I pull off a flawless event, he's always riding me hard with things I could improve on." She shrugged. "It's just his way."

"You spend a lot of time trying to make him happy?"

She barked out a harsh laugh. "Oh, only my whole life. Dancing was uncivilized, so I stopped the lessons. Everything has to be just so. Color is vulgar, so I stopped wearing bright colors."

"Tell me something."

She looked up from her drink. "Yeah?"

"If you can't make him happy, and you're making yourself miserable, why not do what you want to do?"

He had a point. But she wouldn't tell him that. Instead, she followed him out to the pool area and noticed the signs that said no swimming unless there was a lifeguard on duty. "What are we doing up here?"

He stripped off his shirt, nearly causing her to swallow her tongue. She might have already seen all he had to offer, but that didn't mean it wasn't nice to look at. "If I'm lucky, helping you cross off something else on your thirty list."

How in the world did he—

He smirked. "A woman as controlled as you are would have on her Thirty list things she sees as challenges. Probably working her way up to the most challenging. The most basic ones would have to include public nudity. So what do you say, Jai? You up for a little skinny dipping?"

TEN

THERE WAS A GOD. AT LEAST, ALEC HOPED THERE WAS ONE
who would give Jaya the nudge to go skinny-dipping. He tossed
his shirt onto one of the lounge chairs. Watching Jaya carefully,
he prayed she'd join him. Not because he wanted her to break
her rules, though that was a part of it, but because he wanted
her to loosen up. Yesterday she'd been fun and vibrant and flirtatious. Today she was like a whole different person. This
person was cute and he enjoyed teasing her, especially when
she jotted something on that 'to do' list of hers. But if she were
more carefree he could absolve himself of any guilt about getting
too close to her. It was the guilt that always killed him. That
always reminded him he was just like his father.

"Can I take some guesses as to what's on this Thirty list of
yours?" He winked at her and she rewarded him with another
flush. "I've already guessed one thing. Skinny dipping." God, he
prayed he was right about that one. He'd only caught a quick
glimpse when it fell out of her purse. Getting to see that
expanse of pretty brown skin would be heaven sent.

She shook her head, her thick dark hair falling over the

shoulder. "No. Don't bother. You'll never get it right. You don't know me well enough."

Man, he loved a challenge. "Oh, don't I? I know what makes you smile when you're not thinking so hard about being serious. I know your father makes you crazy and I know that even though your sister hurt you, you're willing to try to be there for her. And—" He exhaled. "—I know what makes you come."

Her pretty lips parted as if she were going to say something, then she pressed them together again tightly.

"Fine. I'll go on. I know you've got a steel strength that people probably under estimate. I know that it jazzes you up to make a list. You're hyper-organized but you love super-heroes. I know that even when your world is going to shit, you suck it up and get on with it. I might have only met you earlier this week, but I know a whole lot about you, Jaya Trudeaux. I've been paying attention."

She blew out a breath as she nibbled her lip. "Fine. Skinny-dipping is on the list." She rushed to add, "But just because we're up here at a pool and you've taken off your shirt, which is very distracting by the way, I am not jumping in the pool with you."

"Why not? It's not like I haven't already seen you naked."

She rolled her eyes as she looked around. "You're not seriously going to go in, are you? I don't think we're supposed to be up here." Sniffing, she added, "I'd have to build up a lot of nerve for it, and the point is to sort of have no one around."

"C'mon now. Half the fun is the thought that you'll get caught." He stalked towards her, stopping short of brushing her body with his, his whole body jerking with need. "How about this—I show you how it's done, and then you join me." He eased away from her before he could do anything stupid. *Shit*. Everything from her hair to her eyes to her light jasmine scent made him ache. "I have an idea. Why don't you add skinny-dipping to your list of 'to do's' for the day." As he walked away, he wondered how in the hell he was going to get his pants off without her noticing how massively hard he was.

She shrugged. "I know my lists probably seem stupid to you, but I never get anything done if I don't write it down. Make it a goal. I don't know—it's like I'm paralyzed until I write it down."

"You can do things without writing them down, you know."

She shook her head. "Nope. I can't even get to the grocery store unless I put it on a to-do list for the day. And of course I shop by grocery list."

Alec barked out a laugh. "You mean to tell me you've never been to the grocery store without a list? I'd hate to see that list. No rocky road. No booze."

Her brows drew in. "Not rocky road. Cookies and cream. That always makes my list," she sniffed.

He grinned. "Well you can't be too uptight if cookies and cream makes the list."

"I'm not uptight. I'm just organized and have a plan for life."

Alec grinned. He'd feel like his head was in a noose if he had to live like that. *Kind of like now.* He had too much of his father in him. Needed to be free. *I just want to be free.* Max's words came to him in a rush. Well, didn't the need for freedom run in the family? But he wasn't like his brother. He kept his commitments. He just knew better than to make too many. Alec knew Westhorpe blood ran in his veins.

He wasn't capable of long-term commitment. *Then why do you expect it from your brother?* He also thought about Adele's words, "You are your actions and not your legacy. You can make the choices."

Jaya was more than her to-do lists. Maybe—No. He shook his head. He was about the fun. He wasn't the stick-around guy. He'd proved that time and again. It didn't matter if Jaya made him want to stick around for it. He knew the pattern. He'd eventually get bored and leave.

"Earth to Alec." Jaya waved a hand in front of her face. "You there?"

"Um, yeah," He smiled. "I'm here. So how about I help you with your list. Even if you won't tell me everything that's on it. How about you tell me one thing, and I'll get you to cross it off. You don't even have to tell me how long the list is."

She inched closer to the pool. "Why would you think you're the person to help me?"

"Because, if something made it on there, it's probably a little rash, dangerous, or exciting. I'm the master of excitement."

She laughed, and Alec's heart jumped. He loved the way she laughed. It made her sound young and un-jaded. Her almond-shaped eyes vanished into creases. He couldn't help but smile back at her.

"The master of excitement huh? Not all of my goals are exciting. Some have to do with me standing up for myself."

"Like telling Derrick he was terrible in bed?"

Her eyes widened. "How the hell did you—"

He shook his head and tapped his temple. "Photographic memory. I saw part of your list when you dropped it downstairs."

She covered her eyes. "You're shitting me."

"I shit you not."

Narrowing her eyes, she said, "Prove it."

"Skinny-dipping of course, but to be fair, I didn't see that one clearly. Riding the New York City subway all night, do a round-the-world trip by yourself. Of course those aren't the most fascinating ones. A threesome, Jaya? You honestly don't seem like the girl-on-girl-for-a-thrill kind of person, but if you are, I'm in."

She barked out a strangled laugh. With her mouth agape and eyes bugging, it made him want to laugh. Then, she said the unexpected.

"Who said anything about girl on girl?"

That shut him up. She wanted two men tending to her? Fulfilling her every fantasy? A jealous, possessive lump coiled in his throat. *Easy—you have no claim to her.* Just the idea made him want to kill something, but then the image of her on a bed at the height of ecstasy made him hard. Maybe he could be the guy to give her what she wanted. He was so focused on her fantasy, he only caught the end of her next statement.

"—tending bar."

He blinked for a moment, not understanding the question. Then his brain synapses connected. *That's right, dumbass. She thinks you're a part-time bartender.* She had no idea who he was. And now he'd lied by omission. Clearing his throat, he said, "Yeah, the memory thing does come in handy." Eager to change the subject, he added, "Well, what do we do about this list of yours? You going to let me be the master of excitement of your dreams?"

JAYA BIT her lip as Alec stripped out of his jeans, letting the denim fall to the stone surrounding the pool. Not sure if she should thank the work-out gods or the gods of going commando, she squeezed her eyes shut in an effort to control the moisture pooling in her core.

Holding out his hand to her, he grinned. "What's the matter, don't you trust me?"

"Says the devil as he strips naked." Jaya mumbled under her breath. She didn't know why she was being so stubborn, but no, she didn't trust him. *Let it go, girl.* He'd been nothing but unfailingly nice to her. What was the worst that could happen? "Let's just say, I generally don't trust guys with the devil's good looks and clever tongue to sweeten the sting."

He shook his head even as he clasped his hand around hers. Her whole body jerked from the zing of electricity sparking between them. "You'll like it, I promise." When she still hesitated, he added, "I worked here, learning the ropes of hotel life when I was a kid. Most of the staff is the same. I know the schedules and routines. No one will be coming up to bother us. You're safe here."

Safe. That wasn't a word she was familiar with. But somehow with Alec she felt safe. And that was the real reason she'd slept with him the night before. Why she'd joined him in LA. And why she was about to cross something off her Thirty list. But safe with Alec could be a real problem. She'd start to think safe equated to permanent. And he'd told her who he was.

She already wanted to know everything about him. Things like why he was still a bartender if he had so much hotel experience and a photographic memory. Where he'd grown up, who his family was. But that was the sort of thing you talked about when you were starting to date somebody. Not when he was pretending to be your boyfriend.

Jaya felt the loss of his warmth the moment he released her hand. "How about this—I'll go in and tell you how the water is."

She couldn't help but try to know a little about him. "You never wanted to take all your hotel experience anywhere?"

As he shook his head, water sloshed around him. "Nah. I need to be free. Hotel gigs are kind of permanent."

To Jaya, the idea of rolling from job to job was terrifying. Not knowing where she'd be next. Not knowing how she'd make the rent. But Alec, he seemed like he thrived on it. She wished she knew how to let go like that. Maybe she'd have left Trudeaux ages ago.

"Time's up, beautiful. No one's coming up here. Its shift change time in about thirty minutes. None of the guests come here until it's closer to happy hour. It's just you and me."

Jaya forced herself to turn around. "You'll behave yourself?"

He shrugged. "I'm irresistible. You said so yourself. You might try to jump *my* bones."

Jaya heard the soft splash of water and blushed. She tried not to picture the wide expanse of bare chest she'd seen. Tanned golden skin, begging to be touched. She told herself she didn't care. Didn't want to touch it again. *Live a little, Jaya.* "Fine, I'm coming in, but you're going to have to turn around."

He blinked for several moments as in disbelief. Then a slow sexy smile skimmed his lips and she felt the shiver of anticipation all over her body. He turned around, but not before doing a full perusal of her body. Maybe she'd regret this. Maybe they'd get arrested for trespassing, or public indecency. But maybe, she'd have a little fun.

Slipping off the stilettos, she placed them a safe distance from the side of the pool. She'd flog herself if she ruined them. Stripping off her jacket, she tried to psych herself up for the plunge. "You promise it's warm in there, right?" She heard the low chuckle, and butterflies did the robot in her belly.

"If it's not, I'll help keep you nice and toasty. Body heat is really best for that."

"You wish."

"Yes, I do."

He really was shameless. But it made her feel sexy and daring. She undressed down to her bra and panties and silently thanked the heavens she'd matched today. Red satin covered by sexy black lace. The boy-cut hipsters framed her ass like it was meant to be on display. Though, why she'd bothered to go for sexy over functional she didn't know. *You hoped you'd get him naked, that's why.* She flushed and whispered to herself. "With panties or without? Decisions, decisions."

"You going to take all day, or do you want me to come out and help you in?"

A tiny squeak escaped her lips. If he came out, she'd have a bird's eye view of that sexy form of his. If he came out, they wouldn't make it back to San Diego tonight.

"I'm coming. Just give me a second. So impatient." With her thumbs in the waistband, she took a deep breath. "Now or never, Trudeaux. Shimmy or get off the stage." She shimmied and took a step in the water.

Looking up to make sure his back was still turned, she noticed how the water lapped at his tanned shoulders. It did look inviting. Slipping her bra off, she shivered as the cooling air touched her nipples. Alec was right, the water was warm. Like bathwater and twice as inviting. As she stepped in, every muscle in her body relaxed. *Heaven.*

"See, I told you so." The warm timber of his voice reverberated around her.

When she opened her eyes, she saw he'd turned around, giving her an appreciative once-over. She cringed as she thought of the state of her hair, piled high on her head in the messy knot to keep it from getting wet and going Angela Davis on her behind.

"Okay, fine. You were right. It does feel good."

He winked at her. "You should really listen to me more often. I'm usually right."

She couldn't help but smile at him. "Are you normally so arrogant?"

He grinned. "So tell me, Jaya Trudeaux, how does it feel to cross off something on your Thirty list?" He moved into the shallower water, the pool revealing more of his sun-kissed skin and Jaya's mouth watered. He looked like sin and sex, and she was hungry.

Unsure of him, she mumbled, "What are you doing?"

He stalked closer to her, ignoring her protest. "I'm showing you how irresistible you are."

As he invaded her space, she was forced to use his shoulders to balance, bringing her flush against him. The hard length of his arousal brushed up against her and strained for her touch.

"Shit, Jaya."

When he dipped his head, her heart gave a thud of excitement. Her brain gave a jolt of alarm. Her libido promptly put a muzzle on the alarm bells. Sometimes rules were meant to be broken. As she tipped her head up to meet his lips with hers, a squeak from behind had her cursing. Shoving Alec deeper in the water, she stepped in until the water reached her neck. "Shit. I knew this would happen."

Alec sluiced water out of his eyes. "Relax. It'll be fine."

Jaya couldn't see the person near the door clearly. From the form and movement, she assumed it was a man. "Oh. Hey, Alec.

Sorry to interrupt, but Miss Westhorpe is downstairs. She insists on seeing you."

Alec let out a breath and Jaya could feel the water move behind her as she clutched to the side of the pool. "Thanks, Mike. I'll be right down."

As Mike left in a hurry, Alec reached for her, but she shrugged away. "You should go. I'll meet you downstairs."

"Jaya, I—"

She launched herself up out of the pool to grab one of the fluffy towels on the lounge chairs. Maybe some rules weren't meant to be broken.

ELEVEN

TALK ABOUT DISASTER. JAYA BREATHED A SIGH OF RELIEF AS she let herself into her apartment. The whole damn day was a disaster. Her little jaunt north had not turned out the way she'd expected. After Alec had finished with Adele, they rode back to San Diego in relative silence. She'd been too tired to hold up her end of any conversation.

If she could take an eraser to the last week of her life, she would. Well, okay, not the entire week. Regardless of everything, she'd still had the best sex of her life, and that was nothing to sneeze at. She would still be shut in under her duvet cover with her ice cream if Micah and Ricca had left her to her own devices.

Jaya slipped off the dazzling stilettos and told herself she didn't feel suddenly depressed. She'd had a good opportunity today. One she hadn't planned. One she'd probably blown, but still, a shot was a shot. It was better than what she'd accomplished in the last three days.

Pressing the message light on her answering machine, she padded into the kitchen to prepare a hot chocolate.

"Hey, Jai, it's Micha. Give me a call when you're back."

Of course—there was no way she could vanish with some guy and not have her friends calling for deets.

Another message beep, and her father's deep baritone filled the room. "Jaya, I got your message. I can tell you, I have no idea what you're talking about. I didn't stop you from getting a job. I'm not sure why you think I'd do that or why you think I have time for such machinations. You should call your sister."

When the message cut off, the tightness in her chest was her only clue that she'd been holding her breath. Letting it out slowly, she decided to ignore her father's message. She wasn't in the mood for a fight. Only he could get her this worked up. Only he could make her feel lower than low. She needed to talk to Micha.

Dialing quickly, she sipped her hot chocolate and closed her eyes in bliss as she listened to the ringing. Micha's soft "Hi, Jai," had her frowning.

"What's the matter?"

"I'm unwinding from my day with a large glass of wine. And by glass, I mean bottle. You're welcome to join. You're the one who went off grid today, and you're asking *me* what's wrong?"

"Off grid? What are you talking about?"

"Ricca and I have been calling all day to get the scoop on your man friend, and your damn phone's off."

"Sorry, Alec took me for an impromptu interview in LA."

"Alec, huh? Please God, tell me he was good."

Jaya felt her skin heat as she remembered the previous night. "What do you think?"

"I think you'd better spill the goods."

"Fine, we have a deal. Did you want—" A knock at the door had her getting off the phone. "Hey, why don't I come over in five, and I can give you a brief run down. I'm too keyed up to sit around here."

Hanging up with Micha, she swung open the door.

"Dad, what are you doing here?" He never came over to her place. Not even when she'd moved in. He hadn't been part of the housewarming party. She'd never thought he even knew where she lived.

"You didn't return my call, so I thought I'd come to see you."

Blinking, she clamped her mouth shut to keep from asking why he'd bothered. "I'm sorry, I just got back from LA. I haven't had a chance to even listen to my messages yet." She tried not to wince at the lie. "Can we do this later? I'm on my way out the door. It's sort of an emergency."

Pierre rolled his eyes. "Honestly Jaya a party isn't an emergency."

She took several breaths to calm herself. "I'm not going to a party."

He frowned as he eyed her shoes and all their glittery goodness. "Then where are you going?"

"I need to see a friend. Can this wait 'til the morning? I'll come by the office." She tried to push past him, but he wouldn't let her pass.

"You can't take fifteen minutes to even talk to your father?"

Even before she spoke, she could see the thin thread she'd wound around her temper unravel. "You mean like the fifteen minutes you gave me before you fired me?"

"Stop being childish. I fired you for your own good. You have a lot to learn about clients and their needs."

"You know, you keep saying that and it's weird. Because last I heard, my pitch got you that client. And calling around to make sure I can't get another job is really low, Dad."

He pushed his way in to her apartment. "Why would you think I'd stop you from getting another job? I don't have time for that kind of pettiness."

"Of all the people I've called and emailed, not a single one will even attempt to interview me for a job. Clearly they've had the Pierre Trudeaux treatment. I'm good at my job and you know it. My reputation precedes me, but all of a sudden, I can't get a call back. What am I supposed to think?"

"I don't know why no one will grant you an interview. Perhaps I can make a call—"

"Are you kidding me? You fire me, then tell me I had it coming. But now you'll do me the favor of getting me a job somewhere else. Spare me the favors. I'm going now. The door self-locks so go ahead and show yourself out." Shoving past him, she let herself out of the apartment. She didn't look back as the door clicked softly behind her.

TWELVE

Bleary-eyed, Alec opened the door of his suite to Jaya. "I'm glad to see you don't give up so easily. After I dropped you off last night, I wasn't sure I'd see you again."

Jaya scrunched up her nose. "I don't do giving up. You weren't still sleeping, were you? Come on, it's eight in the morning. We've got plans to make. You can't sleep the whole day a—" She paused as she took full stock of his unclothed form. A pink flush tinged her cheeks. "Oh. Well, surprise."

If she wasn't so cute, he'd have deepened his scowl. Normally, he was a morning person, but the double duty at the bar and corporate offices were killing him. He'd finally hired a manager, so that was one less thing to worry about. But the heaven-or-hell sent dreams of Jaya had made it impossible to sleep. "Didn't close the bar until four." He shuffled into the sleeping area not giving a damn about anything but climbing back into bed, least of all his bare ass.

All he heard from the doorway was, "If you're busy, I'll um, I'll just go and you can—"

He didn't let her finish. Instead, he turned back around,

grabbed her hand and dragged her through the foyer into the darkened sitting area and bedroom. As she attempted to wiggle out of his grasp, he scooped her up in his arms and growled. "There's no one in here with me. Besides, I'm so horny thinking about you, I'd be pretty useless to anyone else. Especially since you've been on my mind nonstop since the other night." He hefted her closer as she stared up at him with those pretty brown eyes. I promise you I'll behave, but if you just lie still and let me sleep for one more hour, I swear we'll plan to your little heart's content. Deal?"

She swallowed hard and then nodded her head. "Can you put me down now?"

He squeezed her tighter, unwilling to let her go. "Yep. Sure thing." When he dropped her unceremoniously onto the bed, she let out a little squeal, which was quickly followed by a groan as he joined her on the bed and hauled her against him.

"Hey, you promised to behave."

God save him from stubborn women. "Yes, I did, and if you just let me hold you like I intended to do the other night, maybe we'll both get some sleep." He anchored her to him and inhaled. *Roses.*

His cock gave an immediate jerk, but he wrestled it back under his mental control with sheer force of will. He honestly did just want to hold her. What the hell was wrong with him? Maybe he'd just change his name to Alec "Sap" Danthers.

If she noticed the unwanted attention of his cock, she didn't say anything. She barely moved. But the longer he held her, the looser her body became until he was pretty sure she was asleep.

Alec drifted into sleep too. Soft material caressing the length of him in such a sweet rhythm threatened to pull him into another tortured dream. His brain issued the command to his hands to rub at his eyes, but one was stuck in an awkward position under his pillow and the other one was too busy stroking a breast that fit his palm like a glove. Not awake.

God, another Jaya dream. All night, dreams like this had kept him up. He'd given serious thought to going to her place last night and telling her the no sex with him rule was stupid. Every time he caught a hint of flowers, he'd been hard. And now he was stuck in another fantasy sure to give him blue balls for life.

Except, this didn't feel like a fantasy. The movements against his crotch reminded him of the way Jaya had moved when she danced. His hips gave an involuntary roll and he hissed when his bare cock came into contact with soft slippery material. Satin, maybe? Like the underwear that Jaya liked to wear. Who gave a shit? A fantasy was a fantasy. Goddamn it. He commanded his eyes to open again, but they ignored him. Most of his concentration was on the soft globe of flesh in his hand.

His thumb circled the tip and he felt it harden. Gently, he plucked at it. The satin around his cock moved again, gyrating in time to his plucking motions. He pinched harder and heard her breath catch. This fantasy was better than the one he had during the night. He could almost feel her breath on his skin. *So real.* His name on her lips brought him closer to waking from the dream, but he struggled to hold on to her.

Maybe he couldn't be with her in real life, but here, hovering somewhere between dreams and reality, just this one time, maybe he could get to release. Get some relief and finally get to sleep. All the other times, he'd been tortured to the point of so-near bliss only to wake with aching balls and no Jaya.

She moved against him, massaging his aching cock with the

satin covered globes of that heavenly ass. He hadn't been this turned on since he was sixteen and Madeline Devon had promised she'd blow him behind the bleachers at school. What was it about Jaya that had him so worked up? She was the sense of stability and normalcy he'd run away from his whole life. He'd only hurt someone like her. Sooner or later, he'd get bored and itchy and need to leave. And she was definitely a picket fence kind of girl.

"Just let me have this one dream," he murmured in an effort to get his body to focus.

Dream Jaya's voice was soft. "It doesn't have to be a dream, Alec. I think I was wrong about this whole not sleeping together thing." Her breath caught as he shifted his hand from her breast and skimmed down over the silk fabric, seeking her center. "I-I can do casual."

He slipped his hand beneath her waistband, traveling over her delicate lips and stroking to find her button. Dipping his long finger into her liquid center, he dragged it through her slick folds until he found his quarry. With firm strokes, he circled the sensitive bud. He'd already learned that direct pressure didn't work, so instead, he teased around it. He knew what she liked.

Moving his hips in time to his strokes he nuzzled her hair. God, he loved the feel of it. So thick and soft. The dark color was like ebony on his pillow. Except he'd never seen her hair on his pillow. The other night, they'd made love in all kinds of places. When they'd finally made it to the bed, he'd shoved all the pillows off the bed.

Frowning, he gave the command for his eyes to open again and this time they obeyed. Cracking them open. Darkness filled his field of vision until he could make out her form. He tested the soft flesh at his fingertips and she moaned his name.

Shit. Not a fantasy. Real life. With the woman who'd said she wasn't interested in a fling. With the woman who made him want to run fast and far. The woman who felt like heaven. "Jai, I—"

"Alec, please, God, don't stop. I want you. I want this."

She trusted him. Again. He wanted to tell her not to do that. He'd only hurt her. But he couldn't form the words. Instead, she moved against him.

"Shit. You have to stop doing that or I'm going to come outside of you instead of inside where I want to be."

She rolled her hips again and he bit out another curse. "I don't care. I just need to have this. Whatever it is. I need it. I need you."

He knew he should stop. Knew if he slept with her again, he was the one in danger of getting hurt. Knew if she begged him again, he might never let her go. "I—"

"Alec." She moaned again.

He stroked her again and felt the flow of juices making her wetter, more ready for him. And he was lost. Shoving aside the scrap of fabric, he nestled his cock against her bare ass and almost came. The contact with her skin felt like he'd been zapped with a taser.

"Alec, I need—"

"I know. I need it too." He shifted her so he could pull her sundress above her head. When he laid her back down, her breasts were free and her back was bare to him save the satin he was working with. As he continued his stroking, he angled her so he could continue playing with her breasts. She tried to turn and face him, but he held her firm in place. "My fantasy. You'll get your turn later. As his cock settled back in position, he hissed when the round tip came into contact with her slick heat.

Resettling the satin in place, he closed his eyes in bliss. With every movement and arch of her back, she milked him with the globes of her ass.

"Damn, Jaya, I've been dreaming about this since the moment I saw you." Pulling away from her, he reached inside the bedside table and fumbled around for a condom while she stepped out of her panties. Making quick work of the foil and latex, he settled back against her to find she'd rolled onto her back. The smile she gave him seized his heart. So bright and so steady. *Oh man, trouble.* How much of an ass was he that he didn't care. All he could focus on was holding her one more time. Feeling her soft skin against his. Never mind that he'd pay for the consequences for the rest of his life.

As he rolled on top of her, she made room for him, even as she hooked her legs around his waist. As she smiled, she said, "Next time I'm being irrational, just go ahead and tell me."

"Anytime," he mumbled against her neck. Conscious thought wasn't foremost on his mind. All he could focus on was the heat surrounding the tip of his cock. He tried to go slow. He really did, but her hands on his ass urging him on were counter to his plan.

"Alec, hurry. I need you."

He clenched his teeth against the roaring need and maelstrom of curses. "Damn it, Jaya, I'm not going to last for more than a minute if we don't slow down a little."

"We can take our time later."

What the lady wants, the lady gets. He slid in to the base of his cock, breath catching in his chest. Beneath him, she moaned out his name. He tried to take control of the pace, but all his attempts to slow down were thwarted by the low keening sounds she made, and the way she traced her hands over his shoulders. Worse was the way she met him thrust for thrust. Rolling her hips, eager to meet his. How she angled her head up and grazed his nipple with her teeth.

"Jaya. Shit." The tingle in the base of his spine was his first warning. The greying of his vision was his other clue. He ground his teeth desperate to ward off the impending orgasm and wait for her. *Wait her out, wait her out. You son of a bitch, wait—*

Jaya's hips bucked and she threw her head back. As she called out his name on a strangled breath, he could feel the walls of her pussy convulse around him.

Her nails dug into his ass and he drove forward, no longer trying to ward off the release. As the zinging pleasure drove him on with each thrust, she locked gazes with him. In that moment, he started to come and poured himself into her soul. Unable to look away, for the first time, Alec knew what true human connection felt like.

"Are you okay?" Still unable to break eye contact with her, he levered himself off her chest to give her some breathing room.

The smile she gave him showed full dimples. The inner walls of her pussy clenched around him and they both moaned. "Yeah. I think so."

She didn't say anything, but he could tell she could feel the change in the air. Something had just happened between the two of them. He didn't know about her, but he was terrified.

"You can use the main bathroom to clean up. I'll use the guest one. There's a blow dryer and toiletries in there if you need anything. Whatever's not in there, I can call down for."

She nodded mutely as she wound the covers around her body. For reasons he didn't want to examine too closely, the shy gesture bugged him. Reaching for the sheet, he tugged at it. "No going back now."

She nodded but didn't release the sheet. "I know."

Tugging harder, the sheet gave way and her breasts spilled forward. Again, his body jerked awake with his cock making a rallying cry. "On second thought, maybe the sheet is a good idea for now."

As she strode off toward the bathroom, she muttered something about incorrigibility.

Alec knew this wasn't smart. He was setting himself up for a hard fall and setting her up for pain. He reminded himself of what would happen if he stayed. How ugly things would eventually become. Jaya Trudeaux had worked her way under his skin. There would be no getting over her now.

After his shower, he ordered breakfast and a change of clothes for Jaya. He'd already snooped in her closet when he hid in her bathroom, so he knew her size. When the bathroom door opened, he couldn't help the excitement at seeing her again. *Easy, Sparky.* But reasoning with Sparky didn't help. He wanted to be let off leash.

She smiled at him as she picked through the new clothes. "You think of everything don't you."

"Well, I had to think fast. I wasn't expecting us to—" He bit his tongue and tried again. "I mean—"

She shook her head. "Relax. I'm okay. I practically begged you to take off my clothes." She eyed his still-shirtless form. "Are you going to finish getting ready? I wanted to go over logistics for the wedding. I made you a folder of the key players. Who you'll need to run interference with if I'm to get a crack at Brett James."

Alec frowned. He knew he was supposed to understand

what she was talking about, but his brain was still foggy. "Logistics?"

Her sunny disposition vanished. "You seriously forgot?"

"It's early. I need a memory-jogger." He shrugged and tried for a charming grin.

"You know what?" she muttered as she dragged on her discarded white sundress, leaving the clothes he'd called up for her in a pile. "Forget it. When you said to come over and give you the run-down, I thought—"

Shit. "Jaya. I'm sorry. I totally forgot. It slipped my mind. And I was up 'til four. Give me five minutes. I—"

"Forget it, Alec I don't need your help. I can go it alone." She slipped delicate feet into her heels.

Her quiet declaration pissed him off. It's not like he was brushing her off. But he had forgotten, so that was a problem. As she tried to move past him to the door, he took her arm. "Look, I screwed up. Okay? I know that. I gave you my word. And that actually means something to me, believe it or not. I said I'd be your date and that's the way it's going to be."

His skin warmed as her eyes roved over his chest. She sighed and relaxed in his grasp. "You're going to need a shirt, then."

He snatched his polo off the bed and dragged it over his head. "Are you happy now that I'm decent?"

She raised an eyebrow. "Happy isn't the right word exactly." She pulled a large folder out of her bag. "So you understand the plan?"

He rolled his eyes as he scrubbed his hands over his stubble. She didn't give up on anything she wanted. And it was exhausting.

He still hadn't had any sleep but at least he wasn't as frustrated now, though the need for her was like a constant ebb in the background. "I understand. I pull your father aside, asking him to show me around the country club. You get Brett James alone and chat with him. Not too hard. If I see Derrick coming, I'll send up the Bat Signal. How did the family dust-up happen, anyway? Your sister seems a little self-absorbed, but man-stealing goes against a sister code or something, right?"

Jaya shrugged. "I guess I bored him or something. All I know is I came home to find Tamara faking it like a porn star in my bed. No surprise really. He was terrible in bed."

"Well, at least there's that. Tamara got what she deserved."

"Can you believe he tried to tell me he thought she was me? We don't look *that* much alike." She blew out a breath and planted her hands on her hips. "Look. I get it. You think this is some 'woman scorned' stuff, but it's really important to me. I need to get my job back."

"I know how important this is to you." He rubbed his hands over her shoulders and she didn't stiffen. "Though I'm still not sure why you have to get *that* job back. If things go well with Adele, you'll be able to get any job you want. Why is that one so important?"

She shook herself out of his grip and he let her go easily. "Besides the fact that Derrick doesn't want me there? This is my family. I belong at Trudeaux. I helped build that place. It's my legacy." She blew out a breath. "It's my home."

A need for home was one thing he could understand. "You can still have a home without being at Trudeaux. Any chance you and your father will work it out?"

"After last night, I doubt it. Without work tying us together, there's nothing really there. After Mom died, he got even more distant. Tams has always been his favorite. But he *needs* me. He just doesn't know it. I promised my mother I would look out for both of them."

Ah, ghosts. She wasn't the first person to do something trying to please someone who was long gone. He lowered his voice. "She's gone, Jaya. Do you really think she would want you bending over backwards and making yourself unhappy? I doubt it."

She softened her chin. "Says the guy who's the perpetual rolling stone and has no responsibilities?"

"Touché." She did have a point. What the hell did he know about family and responsibility? He'd run from everything that ever mattered.

She scrubbed her hands over her face. "I'm sorry. That wasn't fair. I'm really keyed up. I need to make this work."

He shrugged. "But it's the truth, isn't it? I'm the perpetual vagabond. We both know it."

Jaya eyed him shrewdly. "But you don't have to be. You've already shown you're smart. You choose the vagabond lifestyle for a reason." She shrugged. "I wish I knew what it was."

She was digging too close and it made him itchy. No one ever got this familiar with him except Adele, and he'd already worked out ways to avoid her prying. Jaya was something different. She was getting closer to him than he ever let anybody, and he barely knew her. Good thing he wouldn't be here long because she was dangerous to him.

"Jaya, I won't be sticking around."

Her eyes met his. "I know. But there's no point in pretending I'm not enjoying myself."

THIRTEEN

WHEN JAYA'S PHONE RANG FOR THE FIFTH TIME THAT afternoon, she considered putting a bullet through it. She should have turned her answering machine off the moment she got home. Trying to appeal to Tamara's sisterly bonds had backfired on her. She didn't know what had possessed her to try and reason with her sister. All she wanted was confirmation that Derrick had sabotaged her job prospects. What she'd gotten was a fight. Now she had a migraine looming.

Flopping back on the couch, she covered her eyes. Maybe if she continued to ignore the phone it would just stop ringing.

It was either Tamara, who she didn't feel like fighting with anymore or her father who she really didn't feel like talking to. Her father thought cellphones were rude so he didn't ever want to contribute to their noise. Tamara knew Jaya would screen the calls on her cell. Tamara likely didn't factor in the caller ID on the home phone. But whatever. As Jaya sunk further into the couch with her mug of hot cocoa, she tried not to think about what a disaster her life had become. Her cell buzzed with a text message as the voicemail kicked into her land line. "Jaya

Trudeaux, this is Adele Westhorpe's assistant calling. She would like you to meet with her in her office on Thursday at one PM. Please do not be late. Mrs. Westhorpe does not appreciate employee tardiness."

With a frown, Jaya sat up. *Yeash!* What the hell had she signed up for? Then the word employee filtered into her consciousness. *Employee.* Holy shit. Adele Westhorpe was offering her the job.

Her thudding heart threatened to beat out of her chest and her throat constricted. Even with the blown interview, she still got the job? Maybe Alec had intervened for her. Though as he was a bartender and Guy-Friday he hardly had the kind of clout needed to get her a job. With sweaty palms, she carefully placed her mug of hot cocoa on her coffee table. Unable to resist, she stood up and employed full booty dance maneuvers. Finally, she had something that was hers, no Tamara involvement whatso-ever. *And* she hadn't needed her father's connections.

A sobering thought slapped her in the back of her head. If she did this, then it meant she was no longer part of Trudeaux. She was on her own. What if she couldn't— she shook her head. She *could* do this. She was good enough to do this. All she had to do was stay on Adele Westhorpe's good side. How hard could that be?

All she had to do was pretend Dragon Lady was the male version of Pierre. Lord knew she'd had enough practice trying to please someone who didn't want to be happy. And this job didn't have to mean she'd give up her goal of Trudeaux. She'd be on board as an independent contractor. And Adele Westhorpe might not know it yet, but she was just the kind of client Pierre would love. He'd see it as major cache and hire her back in an instant.

Her mood on rocket boosters, she twirled as she scooped up her cell phone off the coffee table. Checking the text message, she couldn't help but smile. Alec.

We should review the plan for the rehearsal dinner. Want to come over?

If he was so kind as to offer her some help, how could she turn him down? Not to mention that her heart skipped at the thought of seeing him again. Those damned butterflies. It wasn't like she didn't know better. "He's not staying, Jaya. No attachments." He'd been clear with her. And she'd been clear with him. She just hadn't been so clear on how he made her feel.

To remind her again why he was on her no go list for emotional entanglements, she pulled up her list of all the reasons why she could not go gaga over Alec. One, she did not have time for a boyfriend right now. Especially now that she was working for Adele Westhorpe and even more so when she got her job at Trudeaux back.

Two, he was not sticking around. As boyfriends went, it was good if they had some roots. Three, he was a sex God. And so good-looking it hurt to look at him. A guy like that would eventually cheat. And next time she couldn't recover.

Four, she liked him, even though he was a sarcastic, slightly pompous ass who was entirely too reckless with his life. She'd vowed to not care about someone more than they cared about her ever again. Five, he drove her bat shit crazy with his complete and utter lack of forethought or planning. Six, she drove him crazy with her complete need for planning and structure. Seven, she liked him. So what if she already wrote that down. It was a good reminder that liking him was a bad idea... just 'cause. Eight, he was really sweet. And made her feel like she was the only woman in the world. She needed to remind herself that men lied. Point blank. She could not trust anything he said. But what about what he did? Slamming the thought shut in a lock box, she peered at her list. This was good. She needed the reminder that he was just for fun. Nothing wrong with a little fun. A little fun to work out the kinks. Totally casual.

She repeated her reasons again. Huffing out a breath, she realized how screwed she was. She was already willing to make up any excuse to go over and see him. And a "thank you for getting me that job" reason was as good as any that she'd already been able to come up with.

Maybe it was time to relax her rules. So far they hadn't gotten her anywhere except heart broken and fired. What was the definition of insanity again? Why did she think she was going to get different results if she kept trying to do the same exact thing? Oh, she'd still go to the wedding and she'd still talk to the client, but not so she could go back to Trudeaux. Not for her father. For her. It was about time she started looking out for herself and doing things just because she wanted to.

Starting now, she was going to start living a little by the seat of her pants. In a hurry to get to Alec, she flitted to her bedroom and kicked off her bunny slippers. Now what did one wear for seduction? It wasn't like she was going to completely abandon who she was. Besides, any good seduction needed a really good plan.

"SO WHAT'S THE EMERGENCY?" Alec let Adele into his suite. "I'm supposed to be somewhere in an hour. I already told you, I don't have any additional information on where Max is.

Caleb's on it." He stopped when he saw the strained expression on her face.

"There was a visitor at the house last night. Several, actually."

"What the hell do you mean, a visitor?"

"One of those low-life goons your brother owes money to came to the house in La Jolla, looking for Max. They paid a visit to Sue, as well. She called me in a panic after they threatened her and the baby then left."

Holy shit. "Where was your security team?"

"I don't need them in my own house. The system was on, but they must have disarmed it."

That didn't sound like any kind of goon he'd heard of. After chasing his brother down in LA, he had taken care of Max's debt in the hopes of accelerating the Max cleanup effort, so who the hell was paying visits? "Are you okay? They didn't hurt you, did they?"

She sniffed and wrapped her arms around herself. "Don't I look fine?"

"No arguments, Mimi. I'm having Caleb put some men on you and Sue. At least until I can find Max. Did they say anything last night? Give any indication of what they were looking for?"

"None of it made any sense. They just kept saying they just wanted back what my son took from them. 'We've moved the cash, but we want our file back. No questions asked if he gives us what we want.'"

"It would make it a hell of a lot easier if we knew what they were talking about." Alec wrapped his arms around her. "I need the video footage from last night. I'll take care of it. I promise."

Her shoulders relaxed a little. "I'm not worried about my

safety. I'm pissed off. I've been dealing with thugs like that half my life. They're usually wearing nicer suits, but I know how to handle myself." The determination and grit woven into her age lines reminded him she was a fighter.

"I hope nothing has happened to him." The quiver in her voice was unmistakable.

Alec knew where she was going. And he wished she didn't have to deal with this. Max was her son and she wanted to protect him. But she knew the situation Max was in and made no bones about it. She knew what could happen if they didn't get him home soon. "Mom, I promised you I'd get him home safe, and I will. You can count on me." It took him several moments to realize he'd said Mom instead of Mimi or Adele.

She must have noticed too, because she waited several beats to respond. "I know I can count on you."

Damn. He didn't want to get into their tortured family stuff now. Jaya was on her way over and he didn't need to be emotionally raw. Brooders were no fun. "I'll let you know as soon as I have a lead."

As she turned to leave, she scrutinized him, taking in his freshly washed hair and looking around the suite. "I interrupted something."

Man, she was quick. "Nope, going out, that's all. You've had me running around so much, I'm taking a night off." His phone chimed and he knew it would be Jaya confirming their date, just like she always did. Another one of her quirks he was getting used to.

"What's your fascination with the Trudeaux girl?"

Alec pinched the bridge of his nose. God help him if Adele decided to butt her nose in. "No fascination, Mimi. She's a friend." He could hope all he wanted, but there was no way she would let it go.

"When you said you found me an event planner, she wasn't what I was anticipating. I expected willowy, earth shatteringly beautiful, blonde and not so bright."

He bristled. "I don't only associate with models."

She chuckled. "Relax. I'm teasing. And I'm not implying she's not beautiful. She is. Especially with that gorgeous complexion of hers. She's just a tad more substantial than I expected. Also a bit of a klutz. But she has fire and determination. And so organized it makes even my eyes cross."

"I don't care if you think she's beautiful or not." Although he did, sort of. If he'd been the kind of guy to bring a girl home, he'd want Mimi's buy-off and respect.

"Of course you don't. I know you think I'm butting in. But I—"

"Did you give her the job?" he interrupted.

"Touchy, touchy. Whether or not I give her the job has nothing to do with you, right?"

He let out a long breath. If Adele wanted to string him along, he wasn't in the mood. "If you say so. You'll do what you want but when you do hire her, don't treat her like you treat your other assistants."

Adele laughed. It was a sound, clear and deep, unexpected and genuine. "You do like her. Will wonders never cease?" Laughing again, she added, "She can take care of herself. She's not some meek little thing who needs you to protect her. Besides, she's smart so she has nothing to fear from me."

As Adele sashayed out of the suite, Alec wondered where he would have ended up without her influence. Somewhere he didn't want to think about.

Not five minutes later, at the knock on the suite's door, his palms got sweaty. He looked down at the offending limbs and rubbed them on his thighs. Why was he nervous? He wasn't seventeen with his first girlfriend. He was grown. Done enough things with women to make Casanova blush.

But Jaya's flirtatious text earlier sent his heart thudding in his chest. *Schmuck.* He had it bad. He'd been all kinds of a moron to think there wasn't anything serious between them. He should have known on that damn elevator and gotten the hell away from her as quickly as possible. But no, he'd let that voice of hers tempt him into talking that night at the club.

At the memory, his body responded. Blood settled in his cock arming him for battle, so to speak. He blew out a breath and reached for the door. She was just a woman. He'd had dozens. But none of them had her humor, her determination. Her endless lists. How in the world could it be that he found her ridiculous list-making the sexiest thing about her? Probably the way she chewed on her bottom lip every time she added something else to her to-do list. He groaned and drew in a deep breath to settle himself. *Get a grip. You'll scare her off.*

Because even though her *I've got a surprise for you* text was flirty, she'd already made it clear she couldn't handle anything more than a fling. Problem was, Jaya Trudeaux wasn't the fling kind of girl. She didn't go around having one-night stands. Or in this case two-week stands. And he clearly wasn't a relationship guy. He knew it better than she did.

Opening up the door, he gave her a smile that said, *no, I haven't been standing on the other side of the door trying to compose myself for the last thirty seconds.*

"Hey." she beamed up at him. "You going to keep me in the doorway, or can I come in?"

Could she come in? His brain tried to work through her words, attempting to decipher into a language he understood. Her voice, as always, melted him and his brain didn't quite kick in the way he hoped. Even wrapped in her Burberry trench and those heels of hers, all he could do was think about her glorious brown skin and how soft it was.

He cleared his throat. "Yeah, of course." A giggle escaped her lips and his brain skipped again. What had he been saying? Eventually, she reached out and gripped his shoulders, moving him aside.

"What's gotten into you today?" Her eyes widened even as her brows drew down. "Shit, when you said come over, I thought—" She looked around and her eyes fixated on the La Perla negligee on the chair. Eyes wide, she met his gaze briefly before making a dash for the door.

Confused, he stared after her, but then blocked her path as dawning hit. "Hey, relax. It's for you. I know it was probably a little impulsive. There's no one else here. You're not interrupting anything." He could have kicked himself. He'd pretty much recreated the scene of Derrick cheating on her. *Stupid, schmuck.*

Her shoulders relaxed and she let out a breath. She rolled onto her toes, then back on her heels. "I don't have some sort of claim to you. I know that. I just saw the lingerie there on the chair and, well..." She trailed off and ran out of steam.

Well done, Alec. You've cocked it all up. "Okay, totally my bad. We can get rid of the lingerie. No problem."

She slapped him on the arm. "Don't be crazy. That looks like La Perla. If you want to see me in it, I can at least try it on."

He grinned. "Can I actually watch you put it on? 'Cause God, what a turn on."

She giggled and his whole body warmed from the inside. "Done deal. But first, I have news."

He drew her into his arms and nuzzled her neck. "Do you now? Does your news involve you going commando under this trench?"

Jaya raised an eyebrow and played with the sash at her waist. "I got the job. Adele called right before you texted me." She did a little pirouette and added a booty shake to that right before she launched herself at him.

He caught her, holding on for a moment too long as his body tensed from the contact. What was he doing? Torturing himself. *Masochist.* "You look happy."

"I'm thrilled. I mean, I couldn't believe it. Her assistant called me, of course. Not like she could ever call me directly. She's Adele Westhorpe, after all, but it's crazy. I start on Monday. I'm so nervous."

He watched her stalk around the room chattering as her words spilled out faster and faster. She really was something else. She was beautiful, but not in the overtly obvious way of southern California girls. He wished she could be his. Wished she were his. "Does this mean operation Trudeaux Events is on the back burner?"

She shook her head. "God, no. It was wrongful termination at the very least. Either way, they need to eat some crow. But I have a life to live. I can't just wait 'til I can get Dad to hire me back." She continued, some of her excitement ebbing out of her. "So anyway, I've been thinking that maybe this whole time, I've been too rigid. Maybe you're right."

He blinked. Frowning. "I'm right about a lot of things. Which item in particular?"

She rolled her eyes. "You know, how you said the other day

that I needed to have some fun and relax. Stop living by my lists and my rules all the time. Go off map."

He'd said that? Well that was before he realized that's what made her fun and interesting. "Hmm hmm."

"Well you were right." Grabbing onto the tie of her trench, she tugged. As the lapels peeled away, acres of beautiful mahogany skin were revealed. All he could do was stare. All moisture left his mouth. The burning in his chest told him he'd forgotten to breathe.

NO MORE LIVING in a fantasy world. It was time to deal with the remains of her life. As Jaya let herself into her condo, her eyes immediately went to the box of things Tamara had brought over from Trudeaux. Most of it could go. She'd rescue her figurines and her software files, but the rest of it she didn't need. She was starting over fresh. No need to bring the past with her.

She tossed her purse on the coffee table and hummed a little tune as her text message alert went off. Probably Alec, finally awake and realizing she was gone. He wouldn't like that. Letting out a chuckle, she snatched her phone up. Ever since that first night, he hadn't been able to let go of the fact that she'd snuck out of bed. It had probably never happened to him before. He was the person who did the leaving. Just like he would this time.

Stubbornly, she shoved the thought out of her head. *Just a fling.* Checking the text message, she smiled.

You abandoned me again.

She texted back. *It's not abandoning if I give you a blowjob before I leave.*

A chime filled the air. *You didn't give me a chance to return the favor. I'm very good you know.*

Jaya's fingers flew over the touch pad as she smiled to herself, enjoying the opportunity to flirt. *Oh I remember. Besides, you passed out and I needed to start my day. Can we meet up later?*

Yes. If you promise I can make it up to you. Late lunch, maybe?

Jaya told herself she should be keeping herself at an arms distance. But she couldn't stop the giddy feeling. She knew falling for him wasn't a smart move. The way he lived his life wouldn't last him forever and it would give her fits if they were together. Someday he'd have to grow up with a real job and a planned future. If only he'd let her help him. *Moron.*

As she hauled the box off the counter, her main line rang and she put it on speaker. "Hi, Micha."

"How did you know it was me?" her friend asked, sounding annoyed.

"You're the only one I know who's up at the crack of dawn like I am. And if by some miracle, Ricca were awake at this time, she'd be mortified to call me before eight-thirty."

Micha chuckled. "Ah, Ricca and her manners. That's how she misses out on good juicy sex stories."

"Who says I'm telling you anything?"

"The way I figure it, you owe me. I called you back yesterday to apologize for my shitty mood from the day before, but you weren't home all day. And your cell kept going to voice-mail. So I figured Alec Danthers struck again and was holding you captive underneath him."

Jaya could feel her skin get hot even as she stammered, "Th-that is none of your business."

"Oh, come on," Micha wheedled. "Some of us have had a dry spell."

Jaya barked out a laugh. "I can't help you if that dry spell is self-imposed. You're perfectly capable of getting someone hot to shower you with affection. What happened with Alec's friend from the bar?"

"Yeah, well, turns out Caleb--that's his name by the way--Caleb. Now lives next door."

Jaya choked on her coffee. "Oh, shit."

"Right back at'cha sister. And to make matters worse, I can see straight into his bedroom window."

Jaya's put the coffee down lest she burn herself. "Double oh, shit."

"Tell me about it. Two nights ago, I—" She paused to clear her throat. "He was Um—I watched him self-gratify." She said carefully.

"Whoohoohoo hoo!" Jaya catcalled. "No way. You did not."

"To make matters worse, it's all I can see every time I pass him in the hallway."

Jaya picked her jaw up off the floor. "Well, what are we talking here? You going to need the cheap drugstore brand of condoms, or will you need to upgrade to magnums?"

"Magnums, for sure." Micha chortled. "Good thing I'm stocked."

"Was he alone?"

"Yeah. It was after the other night at Synthesis."

"When are you going to put you both out of your misery and sleep with him already?"

"Just as soon as he stops insisting on making a whole relationship thing out of it. The other night I tried to take him home and you know what he said? That he wanted to take me to dinner first."

"The nerve." Jaya chuckled. "Do you think he was thinking about you?"

Micha scoffed, a soft growl coming through the phone. "God, I hope so, 'cause that shit was hot."

Micha had been allergic to relationships since Jaya had known her. "Only you, Micha. So guess who has a new job?"

"What?" Micha squealed into the phone. "You got a new job and you bury the lead like that?"

"Well, you distracted me with all that talk of hot sex."

"Who's it with? Please tell me it's Trudeaux's biggest competitor. That'll really show them."

"No, I wish. It's for Adele Westhorpe. She gave me the job."

"Holy, shit, Jaya, that's awesome."

Yeah, it was pretty awesome. And lucky. She had a mortgage payment to make in two weeks. She really didn't want to dip into her savings until it was absolutely necessary. "Now I just have to do a good job."

"Oh, you will. Stop worrying. You were made to do this. I've never met anyone more organized. Even your figurines are organized."

Jaya chuckled. "Most people just call it OCD."

"Well, maybe a little."

"I can plan the gala, no problem. I'm excited to do it. I can really show off my skills. And hopefully Dad hasn't scared off any connections."

"Did you ever get to talk to him? Was he sabotaging you?"

"He says no, but I don't believe him. Wouldn't be the first time he's torpedoed me to teach me a lesson."

Micha was silent for a moment. "Well, he certainly has his own unique parenting style."

"Is that what we're calling it?"

"Wait, is this the annual Westhorpe year-end gala?"

"Yeah, it's the fiftieth anniversary or something, so a pretty big deal."

"Hell yeah, it's a big deal. I'm going to cover it for the magazine."

No pressure or anything. "Well then, I'll have to do a bang up job so you can see me strut my stuff."

Micha rambled on about her new nemesis at work. Jaya went through the box Tamara left her, carefully setting her figurines on the coffee table. Frowning, she searched the bottom of the box, eventually giving up and dumping the whole thing out.

"What is all that noise over there?"

"No. Sorry. Just going through my get-out-of-Dodge box finally and my damn software isn't here."

"Wait, the program you hired that developer to build? The one that took you months to design with the contractor? Ricca and I didn't see you for ages because of that thing."

"Yeah, the same one."

"Oh honey, no." Micha said. "It's not Trudeaux proprietary software. You hired the developer yourself. Shoot, you built it practically. It doesn't belong to them."

Jaya told herself to calm down. It was probably a mistake. All she had to do was call and ask for it back. "I know. I was such a mess, I left all the stuff in my office. When Tamara dropped off my stuff, I assumed it was in there. But I've looked everywhere."

"That bitch."

"No arguments here."

"What are you going to do, besides beat your sister's scrawny ass?"

Jaya had to smirk. Micha was one friend you wanted when you had a body to move. "Don't know. I can contact the developer. I know he probably kept a copy of the work. Or he can at least help me retrieve it."

Micha was quiet, which usually signaled trouble. "You have to go back and get it."

"I was fired, remember? I can call them for it, but I doubt they'll just give it back to me."

"Give it back? Hell, you've got to start thinking like the woman in control you are."

Jaya's eyes squeezed shut. This was trouble waiting to happen. "Are you talking sneaking in and stealing it back?"

Jaya could hear the smile in Micha's voice. "Why would I suggest such a thing? It's not stealing if it's yours."

Her friend had a point. "You know, I might have just the guy to help."

FOURTEEN

TIME TO FOCUS. ALEC KNEW HE'D COME HERE WITH A JOB to do and so far all he'd managed to do was wear himself out with Jaya. Another night like the one they'd had, and he might not be able to stand on his own. But if he had to die from exhaustion, then what a way to go. He bit off a curse at his body's instant response at even a thought of her. "Down boy," he grumbled.

This was a disaster. He had it bad. And any thought he had of getting her out of his system was long gone. There wouldn't be any getting her out of his system. He was doomed if he kept this up. But he'd given her his word. He couldn't just back out because prolonging things would get messy. He was a big boy. He could deal.

With heavy legs, Alec trudged to his temporary office, only to find Caleb waiting for him in the hallway. All he wanted to do was sit down and rest his head for a damn minute. After Jaya had left in the morning, Adele paid him a visit with the Westhorpe financials.

"I would have waited inside, but apparently the security has been updated so my all-access pass has been revoked."

Alec smiled. Caleb's security expertise had helped them counteract some of the more sophisticated key-copying software. "Well, we've got to keep the criminals out, don't we?" Alec let them in and tossed his keys on the oak monstrosity in the middle of the room. "So what do you need? It better be good. I have a shit-ton of work to do."

Caleb's sharp gaze fell on his. "Well aren't you full of piss and vinegar? My guys have Adele and Sue covered. They're safe, and we're getting closer to finding Max. You should be sleeping better. Your girlfriend giving you grief, is she? Has she planned out your wedding yet?"

"She's not my girlfriend," Alec growled, then forced himself to relax his shoulders. "I'm just doing her a favor. And she's doing me one too. Adele gave her the job for the gala. If it takes some stress off of Mimi, that's huge to me right now."

Caleb just grinned. "And just how does she feel about you leaving? Or the fact that you're a Westhorpe? Oh wait, that's right. You haven't told her."

Alec felt like someone was pounding him between the eyes with the sharp end of a hammer. "That's because I'm not a Westhorpe. And she knows I'm going and it's fine. I'm on the up and up, Caleb. I'm not like Dad and Max."

Caleb's smiling face went solemn. "No one was saying you were."

"And what about you? What happened with that friend of hers? The tall one with the..." He let his words drop off.

Caleb closed his eyes and let out a breath. "The seriously excellent rack?" He shook his head. "Nothing happened. She shot me down."

"Makes no sense. She seemed interested."

"Yeah, well. She was interested. Just not in having a conversation with me."

Alec chuckled, even though it made his brain feel like it had been trampled by elephants. "I don't see the problem."

Caleb rolled his eyes. "This from the guy who's spent the past several days holed up in his room with one woman. I don't think I remember that happening—ever. Doesn't seem like you, bro. You took her all the way to LA to meet with Adele."

"I went to look for Max. Adele happened to be in town so what better reason to get her off my back about this damned gala? I brought her an event planner."

"Yeah. Whatever you say." Caleb's grin grew wider but he didn't say anything else.

"She's great. A bit uptight and anal-retentive, but she's sweet and something so—" It took him several seconds to come back to the conversation. "She's not my girlfriend."

"Uh-oh, the great Alec Danthers is going to be sidelined by a woman. They must be making snowballs in hell."

Alec sneered at his friend. Caleb could be a full-on jackass when he wanted to be. "What are you doing here annoying me? We weren't supposed to meet until later this afternoon."

All hint of teasing and laughter vanished from Caleb's face, turning it into an expressionless mask. "Yeah okay. I've got my guys doing everything they can to find your brother, but he's gone full Houdini on us. He must be using cash and driving because we've got no hits on his credit cards and he hasn't tried to board a plane. Since he's not under arrest or technically missing, I'm not having any luck using legal parameters to track his cars."

Alec shook his head. "Don't bother. He left all his cars

either here or at the house in LA. He's probably borrowing a friend's."

"Any chance he borrowed one of the hotel cars?"

"Nah. They're all equipped with GPS and right now they're all accounted for."

"Sorry, man. We'll keep looking."

Alec shrugged. He knew his brother. "It's Max. He'll turn up eventually. He's just being a Westhorpe. The real question is if he'll turn up before those idiots scare Adele again."

Caleb nodded. "We'll keep looking." He rocked back on his heels as he shoved his hands in his pockets. "I have some other news for you."

Alec brought his head up. "What is it? From the look on your face, it can't be good."

"It's not. It's all kinds of a shit show."

Perfect, just what Alec needed. "You mean worse than the current shit show of my life, with bookies after my brother if he doesn't pay and threatening Mimi if she can't find him? This I'd love to hear."

"Your brother's in worse trouble than you thought. Probably worse than Adele knows. There's a reason he's drained his trust fund. You said you paid the bookie after Max? Turns out that bookie works for the Sandovals. As in the Sandoval cartel. And, they think he took something from them."

Ho-ly shit. "Who the fuck would steal from a cartel?"

Caleb nodded. "The other night I grabbed a license plate number off of Adele's video surveillance. Registered to Eduardo Sandoval. My guys lifted some prints and ran them. Those guys were definitely looking for something."

Alec began to sweat. He'd gone to school with Alejandro Sandoval. If evil was an inherited trait, Alejandra Sandoval was the living, breathing evidence of it—as a kid he'd gotten off on torturing other kids. "What the fuck did Max take?"

"I'm working on it. My guess is that Max isn't quite that dumb. Though be might be dumb enough to run drugs through the hotels. I can't prove it yet, though. He might have taken evidence of those transactions. My guys have been hearing that there's infighting in Sandovals gang. One of the guys could have taken something to make a play but hasn't pulled the trigger yet. Max was just an easy scapegoat. My guess is, Max cleaned out his account to give him some running money."

A low whistle escaped Alec's lips. "So my brother's not just a stupid, selfish screw-up. He also has a death wish."

Following his conversation with Caleb, Alec had taken another look at the financials Adele had given him. Wednesday nights were a busy night across all the bars. But the numbers were more inflated than the busiest night he'd ever seen even in a New York or Paris bar. He and Caleb needed to scope the bar out and confirm their suspicions. But they wouldn't see much while working the bar.

Luckily, tonight, Jaya and her friends had provided an excellent cover. Micha apparently needed a night out and Caleb was all too happy to oblige. He hoped his friend could keep an eye out while mooning over the Amazon with the prickly personality. Though it wouldn't make much of a difference. Caleb's men were posted throughout the club. He and his friend were only supposed to be an extra set of eyes.

The booming music didn't help the headache he'd been nursing all day. He was jittery and felt cooped up. He'd taken a couple aspirin, but he knew what the real problem was. This doting boyfriend and attentive son routine were getting to him.

"Are you okay? You seem really distracted?" Jaya's warm,

minty breath tickled his neck as she leaned in to speak to him. He had a little trouble concentrating. The plunging-to-the-navel neckline of her white jumpsuit made his mouth water. Like Caleb, he wouldn't have a chance if he looked anywhere but her eyes.

"I'm good. Just been working a lot, you know." At least that was the truth. He'd started losing track of all the lies he was telling her. Every time she asked a personal question, he did his best to give her measured half-truths instead of outright lies. It was starting to wear on him.

She nodded but studied him closely. The intensity of her stare made his whole body stand at attention. Holding his breath and counting to three, he attempted to calm himself down. He was supposed to be working. He couldn't very well drag her off somewhere private.

"Could you two please stop with the 'rip each other's clothes off' looks? It's a little nauseating."

Beckett had pegged him and Caleb with the hairy eyeball when they'd arrived. Granted, it wasn't as bad as the full on confrontational agro, macho shit he was giving Ricca's boyfriend, Charles. Crazy thing was, he had some leggy blonde with him he was all but ignoring.

Whatever. He didn't have time to get embroiled in the group's melodrama. As Caleb got dragged onto the dance floor by the beautiful Amazon, he signaled to Alec to follow.

Leaning in to Jaya's neck, he gave her a nuzzle. "Do you want to show off those dance moves of yours?"

She eyed him warily but followed him out of the booth to join her friend. Before they reached their quarry, she turned to him. "Was this too much? Meeting the whole gang? I know it's way couple-like. And that's not really our situation. I just wanted to hang out, but you've been weird since we got here. Do you just want to go?"

Yes. "No. I'm just distracted." In that moment, he saw one of Caleb's men brush past him and whisper something. "Come on, let's dance a little and have a good time. I just want to forget this week."

"Being a jack of all trades not all it's cracked up to be?"

"Not this week, it's not."

Making it over to Caleb, they danced for a moment. He allowed Jaya to get distracted with booty-bumping her friend before he asked Caleb, "So what's the deal?"

Caleb shook his head. "No deal. No drugs anywhere. Well, one place, actually. In the bathroom, Chase scared the shit out of some college kid with a joint."

"Damn. Maybe we got it wrong."

Caleb shook his head as he dodged a wobbly brunette with a drink. "I don't think so. If I were them, I wouldn't want to risk my money when our dry cleaner's done a runner."

A bust. They'd been so sure. He'd been banking on having something concrete to pin on the Sandovals that would at least get Max out of danger and away from having to make any kind of statement to the Feds. No dice. "So, what now?"

"I'm still working some angles. In the meantime try not to implode. My guys have got it covered."

How the hell was he supposed to relax and just let Caleb handle it? Adele was counting on him. But Caleb knew what he was doing. Alec had to trust him.

In an attempt to take his mind off the madness, he watched Jaya as she danced. With every sensuous wind of her hips, his brain relinquished the worry over his brother and focused on more pressing concerns—whether or not he could gracefully get her upstairs without seeming rude to her friends.

Turned out, he didn't need to worry about it. "Alec, you want to get out of here?" She had read his mind.

He pulled her through the crowd to the back entrance and private elevators. Once the door shut behind them, she whispered, "Does this elevator have a stop button?"

His eyes widened, but he wasn't one to disappoint a lady. He pushed the emergency stop button.

Alec pulled Jaya to him. He gripped her hips, needing to feel her closer. She molded her mouth to his in easy acceptance. Her lips were pliant, needy beneath his. Alec could feel the rise and fall of her breasts with each breath. Feel the heat coming off her body. All he could think about now was how to make her burn hotter.

She moaned against his lips, her body rubbing against his, the friction driving him mad. He pulled the straps of the jumpsuit down, baring her to the waist. When his fingers met the skin at her back, he gasped at the satin feel. He would never get over how soft she was all over.

Her hands clutched at his shirt, impatiently, undoing the buttons. They both struggled out of the rest of their clothes. Her bare breasts swayed with each movement, distracting him. When they were fully naked and he reached for her, his hand trembled as they molded to her breasts testing their weight, the way they fit his hands. The way her eyes darkened to black as she moaned his name. Jaya shuddered as he circled the dark tips.

He smoothed his hands down her sides to her thighs and lifted her until her legs wrapped around his waist. As gently as he could, he lowered them to the floor and searched for his jeans. Grabbing a condom, he sheathed himself quickly then lay back on the cool marble floor drawing her over him.

Easing her down, he watched in rigid anticipation as he lowered her over him. Her eyes widened and he worried she wasn't ready for him. But then he could feel her mold and stretch around him. The tingling bliss threatening to blind him stabbed at the edges of his vision. "God, you are so tight."

"You are so big."

A rough chuckle escaped his chest, which brought her breasts rubbing against his chest. "You're going to kill me."

Retracting half an inch he grinned as she moaned his name. Surging forward, he shut his eyes, trying to focus, to ward off his impending orgasm. Jaya didn't make it any easier for him. He moved in slow, deliberate motions at first, wrestling her for control. For every stroke, she tried to get him to speed up.

He gave up the battle. He took hold of her ass and squeezed, unable to hold onto control any longer. In two deep strokes, he could feel her buck against him, the tiny tremors starting at her core and radiating through her body. She scored her nails down his chest and he roared with the pain and zinging passion.

He watched as she pinched her nipples and threw her head back. Her response to him was so unfiltered. She held nothing back.

The tremors grew, shaking her body, and she whispered his name again. When she stilled and tensed, he worried for a moment before he felt her pussy clench around him, clamping down on his cock, refusing to release it. Grinding his teeth together, the tap dance of bliss against his spine had him holding her hips against him. Unable to hold off, he roared as the trembles overtook his body and the pleasure darkened his vision. As his body jerked his release, he wished they didn't need the condoms. Wished she could feel the force of his release within her body.

"Jaya, I swear to God, you're trying to kill me."

"Not yet. I've still got a few days left and there are some things I haven't tried yet."

He groaned as his spine got even friendlier with the hard floor. "I can honestly say I've never done this before."

She grinned. "Well, hang on tight, Maybe I could teach you a thing or two. Cross a few things off *your* list."

He could only wish.

FIFTEEN

"So explain to me how when you thought, 'I'm going to break into my old place of employment,' you thought of me?"

Jaya could feel Alec's breath on her as they entered the elevator in the Trudeaux building.

Pressing the button to the top floor, she smiled up at him. "Aren't you the one who keeps telling me I need to be more daring? I'm being adventurous."

"When I said that, I meant maybe go rock climbing with me or something. Not a little B and E."

"It's not B and E if it's my software. They have no right to it. I'm just going to get it back."

He rolled his eyes. "Don't get me wrong. I like this new naughty mischievous streak of yours. I'm just telling you, if we get busted, I'll sing like a bird about how this was all your idea and you strong-armed me."

She hid a smile. Casting him a sidelong glance, she doubted anything could strong-arm him. Not with all that muscle. "I'll keep that in mind."

"It's okay, I'm pretty sure I'll make bail if we get pinched.

And I'm down for anything that might help me get laid by you, but are you sure you want to do this? Maybe it's time to face a new reality, Jaya. Maybe you're not meant to be here at Trudeaux."

She narrowed her eyes at him. "I'm not giving up on what I want. I belong here. Now you remember the plan?"

"If anyone stops me, I act like I'm looking for your office. Make whoever dares stop me have to deal with the unpleasant task of telling me you no longer work there. If they ask questions, kick a major fuss."

"Right. While you do that, I'll just pop into Tamara's office and get what I need."

"And if it's not there?"

She bit her lip. "It'll be there. She stole it. I know my sister. Or at least I know Derrick."

"Fair enough." He rolled his shoulders. "Are you sure you want to do this? We can just push the down button and go back to the car. Maybe you could ask your father for the software."

Jaya clamped her jaw. "And I've told you, he won't give it to me. He thinks I'm doing the spoiled-brat thing. I'm tired of rolling over. Just taking what's mine."

He grinned. "Then I'm behind you. I have a good lawyer on speed dial I did a favor for once." He chuckled.

As they exited the floor, she led him to the guest waiting room.

"Remember, most of the staff is at the marina prepping for the wedding, so it's a skeleton crew. My office is next door. Just whistle or speak loudly as a warning. I'll hide or something. I only need a couple of minutes."

"You know where to look?"

She nodded. "Yeah. Before it was Tamara's office, it was

mine. I doubt she's had a chance to change the safe. If the software is here, it'll be in there. She probably doesn't know how to use it yet."

"You're sure you want to do this?" He peered down at her and searched her face.

"Would you relax? I know what I'm doing."

"As monstrous creations go, you're one hell of a beauty."

The moment Jaya entered her old office, the smell of perfume assaulted her. Of course her sister would turn this place into a girly fortress. *Keep on the task at hand.* She could lament about the unprofessional nature of it after she got what she came for. Lucky for her Tamara hadn't begun a renovation of the office. The layout was the same, meaning the safe was in the same place. Slipping into the closet, Jaya opened the compartment that hid the safe. She tried the original combination. It didn't open. *Damn it.*

She tried her father's birthday then her mother's. Then Tamara's. But as flighty as her sister might seem, she wasn't stupid enough to use her own birthday as the safe combination. Jaya started sweating under the pressure. More than once she had to stop to wipe the moisture off her palms. "Come on, come on. What would it be?"

"What the hell is taking so long?" Alec's voice right behind her had her giving a squeal of alarm.

"Damn it. What the hell are you doing in here? You're supposed to be the look out. How can you be looking out if you're in here with me?"

"It's been more than ten minutes. I figure you'd had some sort of crisis of conscience."

She rolled her eyes. "No. I'm trying to deal with the safe. Tamara changed the combination."

Alec frowned. "Did you try her birthday?"

"I'm not stupid. Of course I did. No dice."

"Any other bright ideas that can get us arrested?"

She hit him on the arm. "What about you? Aren't you supposed to have some tales of a misspent youth or something? Don't you have any safe-cracking experience?"

"Shit, not even I'm that good. What about something important to her? From what I saw, she's all about her all the time, but she seems to love the glory days. Anything from her past that would mean something."

A little light bulb flashed in Jaya's memory. "Of course—why didn't I think of it?" She tried one combination of three numbers, then another. Neither worked. On the third try it finally clicked open.

Alec's eyes widened. "What did you use?"

"Through high school, she had three boyfriends from the moment she could date. Each was captain of the football team at the time. I used their numbers."

"You're kidding me."

She shook her head. "Tamara was on the cheerleading squad. Captain was no less than she thought she deserved." Jaya reached into the safe. There were several papers, the petty cash box—and the flash drive with her software. Snatching it out of the safe she waved a fist in triumph. "Got it. Now let's get the hell out of he—"

A noise in the outer room shut her up. Alec pulled her close and clicked the closet door shut behind him, closeting them in together in the confined space. Her breasts brushing up against him, she sucked in a breath, only to have her nipples rub against his chest.

Neither of them breathed, straining to hear the sounds in

the adjoining room. What the hell was Tamara doing back? She should have been so busy with the planning, she wouldn't have gone anywhere near the office. Unless it was someone else. Though that person had a death wish if she knew her sister. Tamara hated anyone touching her stuff. It was the one anal quality she'd been born with.

"Do you think it's your sister?" Alec's voice was so low, she was only sure of what he said by the vibrations coming from his chest.

She shrugged. "Dunno."

He opened his mouth to speak again and she shoved a hand over his moving lips. They didn't need to be discovered poking around the safe. Her father would for sure have her arrested. Or at the very least, disowned. She heard the chair in the office slide against the hard wood and smack into the window. Damn, whoever was in there, planned on being around for more than a second. She forced her shoulders to relax. If they had to stay in here for a little while, she didn't want cramped muscles as a result. Too bad that was easier said than done. She could literally feel everything about Alec. His breath, his body, his tension, his hands, which settled just above her hips.

Her body screamed for them to do more than just sit on her waist. Her mind screamed warnings. *Danger Jaya, danger. Man too close.* She compelled her brain to force-quit the alarm. That was, of course, until she felt the hard length of him butting up against her. She sucked in another breath. He bit out a low curse through clenched teeth as his hands tightened imperceptibly.

He tried to move away, but that only made it worse, brushing the hard length of him against her abdomen some more. This time she joined him in the cursing. His spicy scent enveloped her and her mouth went dry. The usual cool temperatures of the office felt ten degrees hotter.

He mumbled something that sounded like an apology. She couldn't be sure, as he said it through clenched teeth.

"Let's just think about something else," she muttered, trying not to picture the elevator, her with her legs wrapped around him, begging him to make love to her. Him stroking her core 'til she'd had an orgasm so strong, she'd collapsed. *Stop. Stop it now, Trudeaux. You're not helping yourself.*

"I'll stop thinking about it when you stop looking like you're remembering the other night in the elevator."

For the first time since she'd been wearing them nonstop, her shoes began to pinch and she shifted.

"Jaya, you need to stop moving." Alec's voice was tight.

She understood where he was coming from. This was too much. They'd had sex in numerous positions and all kinds of places, but being trapped in something the size of a coffin played havoc on her nerves. If only he didn't smell so good. If only her whole body didn't itch to have his hands on it. She heard the low moan and didn't realize it was coming from her until she felt his hands on her hips again, rubbing and soothing.

"I know. It's not easy for me either, sweetheart."

"So much for my bright ideas. I can't believe I thought I could come in here and just do this. So stupid." From now on I'm back to following the rules.

Alec hushed her. "It's okay. So it didn't go according to plan. Could be worse."

She would not cry, though tears pricked her eyelids. Stupid stupid stupid. His arms went around her and it was almost worse, because it reminded her of how they'd met. He pulled her even closer and there was no hiding his need from her.

There was also no hiding her response to him as her nipples pressed into his shirt.

Hey, it's not every day I get locked in a closet with a Greek God right? I might as well enjoy it.

He held her head to his chest and stroked the back of her head, still hushing her, still in comfort mode. Until she breathed into his neck. She felt the instant change in him. The tension creeping into his shoulders. The way his hands tightened on her waist. The low rumble in his chest. The hardening of his dick against her. She knew the kiss was coming even before he dipped his head.

For several moments she couldn't believe he was going to kiss her. But she knew. She wasn't that innocent. She was bracing herself. When his lips met hers, it was all she could do not to climb all over him. His lips were soft at first, undemanding. Subtle. Then he angled his head and deepened the kiss. His tongue crept in to meet hers. It teased hers into a dance. Tasting, stroking, begging for an answer. And the answer was heat and sex and need. God, the man could kiss. She moved against him in an ancient need to get closer. Her hips rocked against his and he growled.

"You keep doing that, and your sister's going to hear you screaming my name."

Alec shifted position. Jaya found her ribcage pressed up against a cabinet in the miniscule closet space. Finding her back crowded by a large, hard, very earthy male, she held her breath as the voices in the office drew nearer. She felt Alec's hands tighten at her waist in silent warning not to make a sound, and strained to listen, but the voices were too muffled.

When his hands tightened on her hips again, her stomach contracted. She squeezed her eyes shut, trying to ward off the sensations. She shifted in an effort to create more space between them, but all she managed to do was bring herself closer to Alec —all of Alec.

After that, she tried to keep as still as she could, which proved increasingly difficult as he placed kisses at her temple, presumably to keep her calm. She took deep breaths and tried to think of something innocuous. Though every time she shifted, she could feel the length of him against her ass. She tried to swallow, but her mouth felt like sawdust. The things this man could do to her body by barely touching her. All she could do was brace herself against the safe in front of her. She rolled her head forward, exposing the back of her neck.

She held her breath as she felt the telltale sign of his arousal nudging against her insistently. God, he picked a hell of a time. Heart thudding in her chest, her brain was conflicted.

They couldn't do this here. Though, her body was in no mood to listen to her brain. Why did the one man who could make her feel this way have to be Alec? They had no future. He would leave and she'd be left holding the pieces.

No, for her it had to be *Mr. Handsome as Sin*, who was all wrong for her. When his hands began to move up her ribcage, beads of sweat popped on her brow. Did he have any idea what he was doing to her? She shifted some more, trying to alleviate the throbbing ache between her legs. When she heard his muted groan, she felt a swell of feminine pride.

His hands paused just under her breasts. It was all she could do not to put them on her breasts herself. He beat her to it and gently rubbed her nipples with his thumbs.

Body on fire, she rolled her hips again. What the hell was wrong with her? There they were up shit's creek with no paddle and she was giving serious thought to having sex in a closet.

Her nipples had started to tingle and pebbled into hard peaks. Her thighs quaked with the force of her arousal. Her bones had taken on a jelly consistency.

She had to touch him. Unfortunately, her current position and the need to be quiet limited her options. She twisted her arm behind her. Her palm came in instant contact with his hard, steely thigh. He was solid everywhere, all sinew and stone.

She drew her hand up until she hit pay dirt. He hissed as she stroked him once...twice...three times. She felt him go from firm and interested to rock-hard and relentless. She settled into a rhythm of rocking against him each time he squeezed her tender flesh. She was further rewarded with a feral nip at her neck.

She should have been reminding him that they were in danger of getting caught instead of kneading him to full readiness. She should have been doing everything to keep quiet, not wanting to feel his hard flesh buried deep in her. She wanted him. Her dewy core was already slick in preparation for him. She moved against him again and reveled when he tensed.

Alec let his hands roam back down past the front clasp of her skirt and it was her turn to hiss. His fingers tapped a sensuous rhythm down to her aching core. When he finally reached her strip of springy curls, he paused and nipped her ear. "Stay still and don't make a sound," he whispered. She stilled and his hand continued its journey. He inserted one impossibly long finger into the silken heat and she had to bite her lip to keep from crying out. To reward her silence, the one finger was joined by another, sliding into her in an ancient rhythm.

In a breath the voices drew nearer. Both of them held completely still, save his moving fingers. What a sight they must have been. Her hands behind her, stroking him. His hands in front of her, stroking her.

She was out of her mind. First the Nancy Drew antics. Now this. She'd never behaved like this a day in her life before she met him. She was out of her mind, pure and simple. Clearly this was not the place or the time. But it didn't stop her with Alec.

If either of them made a sound, they would be discovered. Alec was dangerous to her sanity. She should have listened to him. But oh, no, she wanted to follow her heart.

ALEC BLINKED, trying to find some measure of his sanity. With every infinitesimal movement of her hips, he wasn't sure if he was in heaven or hell. He tried to school himself to keep his hands at her waist. Unfortunately for him, his hands hadn't listened.

When she rolled her head forward, it had been a mistake to kiss the exposed skin of her neck. But he'd felt her shudder and the heat rushed through him. And here he was, so desperate to have her he would take any risk.

The voices in the office were muted, but someone was still in there. He made a feeble attempt to gain control of the situation. *Control is all I need.* All he had to do was remove his hands. The only problem was, Jaya kept grinding her butt up against his crotch and his hands had tightened in reflex. His body was enthusiastic, to say the least.

When she'd made that soft huffing sound in the back of her throat, he nearly came. The feel of her against him sent sensual alarms throughout his body. In their current position, he couldn't touch as much of her as he'd wanted to.

The voices moved farther away but not out of range. Alec felt the urgent need in his blood. He tried to support Jaya as she used one hand to brace herself. She brought her other hand around and massaged the length of him again.

He rewarded her with a low groan in her ear. "We have to stop."

Ignoring him, she pumped again. His eyes crossed. The last bit of his control disappeared. He brought his head down and teased her left ear none too gently with his teeth. His hands massaged and kneaded her sensitive breasts. He loved the way they fit his hands. Her nipples responded to his hands like puppets to a puppeteer.

"I want you."

His admission only served to fuel her movements. He felt her delicate hands tighten around him once again and lost it. All reason had long flown out of the window. His fingers retreated, then slid back into her. Her inner walled quivered around his fingers and he murmured in her ear, "Easy beautiful, easy."

When the voices drew nearer, they both froze where they stood. Sweat beaded on his brow and he could have easily died right there and not cared. His dick twitched in her hand and it was all he could do not to scream in frustration.

At the softening of the voices, he breathed a sigh of relief. Alec's mind slowly registered that the voices moved farther away and eventually ceased. There was a soft click of the office door. After that, he heard nothing. His gut told him they might still be there, but his body didn't want to listen.

He felt Jaya relinquish her hold on him, but he wasn't done with her yet. He wanted to hear his name. He *needed* to hear it. He nipped her ear and pulled his already slick fingers from her body, then slid them back in again. He got what he wanted. Jaya bit out a choppy whimper. "Alec."

"Tell me you want me." He was relentless. He kept stroking until her knees buckled.

A soft, "I want you, Alec," came out on a breath. "I want you."

Alec didn't ease up on his caresses. His breathing was as choppy as hers. He felt her quake. His own whispers sounded harsh to his ears.

"Jaya"

"Mmm."

He felt her tense, nearing her climax.

"Baby." His fingers were dripping from her response.

"Oh, G—"

"Come on." His breath ragged. "Let. Go. For. Me."

"I wa—"

"I know." He throbbed with need.

Her last breathy sigh of his name was like music to his ears. "Al—ec." She melted like butter in his arms. His hands steadied her as he tried to think about anything that would abate his arousal.

Jaya was having none of it. With shaking fingers, she continued to knead him.

"Jaya, if you don't stop, I'll—"

"Come?"

"Jesus." He wanted to roar with the frustration.

Alec stopped her roaming hand with his. Certain the office was now deserted, he took as much of a step back as he could manage. Jaya moaned at the separation. He quieted her by massaging his hands over her back. He filled each hand with the soft skirt fabric and hiked it up.

He smiled at her soft gasp when the cool air hit her flesh. Alec groaned when he realized she'd only been wearing a black silk thong and matching garters under her prim skirt all day.

"Alec. What are you..."

He filled his hands with her firm, warm ass and lifted a little, forcing her to bend at the waist and grip the cabinet with one hand for support. With her other hand, she continued her earlier stroking of his cock and he bit out a string of curses. "Jesus, Jaya, I can't hold on if you—"

"If I what?"

In a swift motion, he removed his belt and shoved his jeans down. She gave a soft ooh sound when her palm came into contact with his smooth tip. A small bead of liquid escaped and helped lubricate her palm as she brought him closer and closer to the brink. Roughly, he tightened his grip on her hips and bent her over as far as she could go, forcing her to release her hold on him.

His cock nestled in the cleft of her ass. He leaned over to place kisses on her exposed neck. He fumbled with the foil packet he'd rescued from his wallet and shoved aside the flimsy material of her thong. And then, without preamble, he lined up the head of his cock to her folds and slid in to the hilt, making her groan.

For moments, he stayed just like that relishing the feeling, her inner muscles tightening and massaging the length of him. Those sexy mewling sounds from deep in her throat that revealed she was close to coming began again and they were music to his ears. When he stroked the tip of her nipple, she gasped out his name again as her whole body quaked in his arms.

Taking his cue, he began to slide inch by inch of his cock out of her until he was nearly completely out. He repeated the movement, shallowly penetrated her, in and out, in and out until he made her beg for more.

"Damn it. Stop teasing me.

Chuckling, he whispered, "You want more, do you?"

At her muffled response, he penetrated her as deep as he could go, slowly building tension. Gasping for air, he filled his hands with each cheek and gripping them for support, he loved the way the soft globes filled his palms.

While one hand continued to knead her taut flesh, the other caressed her back, pausing to massage the back of her neck, reaching around to her face to trace a slow line across her bottom lip. She responded by peeking out her hot tongue and drawing in his thumb. As she sucked, deeply, she also grazed the soft pad of his flesh with her teeth.

"Jaya—" he warned.

Removing his thumb from her lips, he brought his hand back to join the other on her ass. With his moist thumb, he traced the line bisecting her soft orbs until he reached his quarry. He circled the sensitive flesh until he could feel her pussy tighten around his pulsing cock.

He knew what to wait for, he continued to tease until he knew she was about to go dancing off that ledge, then stopped his ministrations.

"God, don't stop now," she begged.

Rocking his hips forward, he whispered, "I want you so hot, you can't possibly wait any longer."

He felt her tighten her inner muscles around him and smiled.

Her breath was ragged and her muscles drew him in farther.

"I'm already so hot I can't wait any longer." Jaya rotated her hips, forcing a low moan from his lips.

"Are you sure?" he asked, all the while rocking his hips gently back and forth.

"Yes. And let me remind you, payback is a bitch."

Alec smiled slowly and gave her what she wanted. Continuing his slow circles with his thumb, he gently penetrated the tight ring of muscle. With ragged breathing she pushed back in time to his rocking. Once again he felt the pulsing and quivering around his burning cock as she pushed herself flush against him. His climax wasn't far behind hers. With three long strokes, he exploded, certain his body would come apart at the seams.

They stayed like that for several long moments, chests heaving. Sweat poured from his forehead and he splayed his hands across her back. Alec thought if he could just stay like that for a moment, the blood would rush back to his brain so he could begin to use it.

Gradually, clear reason and thought returned to him and he slid out of Jaya, though that movement was halted by her protesting inner muscles. He moaned. "Sweetheart, we can't stay here like this."

Slowly he helped her right her clothing. He pulled her skirt down and helped her straighten it. Before he turned her around, he managed to get his jeans back on. When she faced him, he saw the residual lust in her eyes. Unfortunately, he also saw a cautious wariness.

Choosing to ignore it, he dipped his head and slid his tongue over her soft, full lips. She responded to him as she always did. When he pulled back, he took in her unfocused eyes and parted lips and wished they had more time. They couldn't stay there like that.

"We have to go."

She straightened with a groan. "What the hell did we just do?"

He bit his tongue before something deep could spill out of his mouth. Telling her he didn't want to leave her would just freak her out. And it wouldn't change anything. He was still a Westhorpe. He was still going to leave. Sooner or later he'd get the itch to go and he would only hurt her.

Instead, he flashed a grin and his teeth ached with the effort as he helped her straighten her top. "We just crossed something else off on your Thirty list."

SIXTEEN

"Are you going to stand there lurking in the corner all afternoon, or are you going to come in and tell me what's bothering you?"

Alec rolled back on his heels but made no attempt to go into Adele's office. How the hell was he supposed to tell her what he'd found?

He told himself he didn't fear rejection once she found out her real son wasn't perfect. Wasn't afraid she'd blame him. *Right. Stop being a pansy ass. Spit it out and get it over with.* "We need to talk."

She slid the glasses off the end of her nose, placing them on the files in front of her. She gave him a sharp, narrowed-eyed look that told him she was as shrewd as always. "Spit it out, Alec. I don't have all day."

That was her way. No nonsense. "I reviewed those files you wanted me to look through." Stepping out of the shadows, he picked a seat directly in front of her. It was Band-Aid ripping time. "I found some inconsistencies with the accounts."

Her face was a mask. No tight drawing in of the eyebrows. No thinned lips. She might as well be wearing a kabuki mask.

"Over the past three years, someone has been laundering money through the hotels. A little here, a little there. Over several different accounts, primarily the club accounts." He let that part hang. He couldn't bring himself to tell her it was accounts Max should have been watching.

"How much?"

"Sum total, just over two million." He waited for the anger or even tears. He'd only seen Adele cry once and even then it had been in anger, over him. It was when he'd shown up on her door step asking to be taken in. She'd railed and screamed at his father, but not because he'd been unfaithful. More because his father didn't want to take him in. She'd cried then. If she'd ever cried after, he'd never seen it.

But not now. She leaned back in her chair, fingers steepled under her chin.

"I'm glad you confirmed it."

He frowned. "You knew?"

"I had my suspicions. Really, Alec, you think there's much that goes on around here that I don't know about?" She arranged the files on her desk. "Every hotel with a club or lounge started seeing more and more losses. I started shutting them down. Except for Synthesis. I didn't know the extent of the damage. Doesn't help when it's lots of cash changing hands."

He shook his head. "It's been killing me trying to figure out how to tell you."

She clasped her hands in front of her.

"You shouldn't have worried. You're not the thief. You didn't take a family business and defile it with drug money."

He shook his head. "But Max did. He's got more problems than you know about."

Waggling a finger at him, she said, "I know all about his problems. No matter what I've done, he's never turned out how I expected. He's spoiled and arrogant and self-indulgent."

He couldn't believe she was missing the bigger picture. "Mimi, it's worse than that. The trouble waiting for him is far worse than what the board will do to him when I bring him home. The Sandoval brothers are bad news. The goon they sent will only come back. They think Max took something from them and they'll do what it takes to retrieve it." He ran his hands through his hair. "You can cover those accounts all you want. But you can't save him from himself."

Her eyes were hard and shrewd. "You don't think I know that? Lord knows I've tried with him, but he's not interested in changing. He has your father's temperament." She shook her head. "I don't know where I failed him."

Alec ground his teeth. "You would have been better off completely cutting him off and sending his ass to military school. But that's beside the point now. Now you have to deal with the mess he made. And it's bigger than you having to cover some accounts or make the numbers add up. If the Sandovals don't get what they're looking for, they'll kill him. Even if he gives it back, they'll still probably kill him. His only chance is to go to the Feds."

She frowned. "I don't think—"

He shook his head. "He's been running drugs out of the larger clubs. So far, I can't find evidence of anything out of Synthesis, but the clubs in La Jolla and Oceanside have been making more of a profit than they should be, while the hotel clubs that are part of Westhorpe are losing money in droves. He did more than run off. He left you holding the bag. The Sandovals have the Westhorpe in their crosshairs and they won't just go away."

Adele didn't even blink, just stared at him long and hard before pushing back her chair. As she stalked to the floor-to-ceiling window overlooking the Gaslamp district, he worried that this would all be too much. Had he gone too far?

"What are you going to do, Mother?"

The look she gave him was quick. He rarely called her mother. It stunned her into silence for a moment. She blinked rapidly, sniffing as she stood up straighter. "I'm going to do what I always do. Deal with him. You bring him home to me, and I'll fix it."

He blinked at her. "How? All due respect, but I don't think you can control him."

The look she gave him reminded him of the time she'd caught him at age thirteen gawking at the naked sunbathers on one of the rooftop spas. She'd grilled him on the finer points of respecting women until he'd been sure to never disrespect another woman in his life.

"I am still Co-founder and President of the Westhorpe Hotels. So take your due respect and shove it. You think I'm so loving I won't send your idiotic brother to jail? You're mistaken." She inhaled and then let out a slow even breath as if she was counting the beats to calm herself. "He stole from me, you, the employees, and for what? To get into bed with the dregs of the earth? Jail's too good for your brother. If I had my way, I'd send him to a Thai prison so deep and dark, he wouldn't see daylight for some time. But I might have to settle for good-old fashioned San Quentin."

Alec shivered. He'd never meant to get her this upset. "Adele, I didn't mean—"

She interrupted him, dismissing his words with a wave of her hand. "Yes, you did. You think I still don't have what it takes to run this place. And yes, I've been a fool, but no more. Let's take care of our immediate problems. The Sandovals."

"We can go one of two ways. Tip the police. Though, if we do that, it'll be in the papers. If we plan to go public in the near future, there will be no way to keep any of this stuff private. Our other option is to just shut down those clubs. Pay off the Sandovals if we can. Make it go away for now." He shrugged. "Both options still mean we have to deal with Max. If you try and cover his ass, it will come back to bite yours."

"What's your recommendation?"

"Close the clubs. Leave Synthesis open to see how it performs. In regards to the Sandovals, I'm still deciding. Caleb is thinking of a way out of that one. As for the public filing, even if none of this goes to the press, you're not ready. Your house is not in order. I say, give it another year while you clean house. You'll need to run it by the board, of course, but it's the safest bet. You can go public next year when your financials are clean."

Adele leaned against the glass framing. "I still need a voice and a VP of Operations. I simply cannot be everywhere all the time. I wish I could change your mind about coming back, but I know better. I've learned my lesson with Max."

He let out a small breath and said quietly, "I'm sorry."

Her voice, usually so foreboding, was gentle. "For what? At least I have one son I can count on."

"You're sure you still want me to bring him back?"

She gave a toss of her head as if she could shake off the

melancholy. "Yes. He has to answer for what he's done." The breath she let out was weary. "I'm sorry, Alec. I didn't want to burden you with all of this. You made yourself clear when you arrived and I was listening. I promise once he's home, I won't tie you here and try and guilt you into staying. This isn't where you belong."

"Adele," he started.

She laughed. "Back to that, are we? I'm not trying to guilt you. It's the truth. I learned long ago that for you to be happy, you had to do your own thing. I respect it."

SEVENTEEN

With jangling nerves, Jaya stared at her quarry.
There he was. Brett James, sitting at Tamara's rehearsal dinner, like part of the family. All Jaya had to do was talk to him and she could have her life back. Could prove that she wasn't a failure. Be welcomed back into the fold.

Except her feet where having a hard time making the trek and it wasn't the fault of those gorgeous four-inchers. She was terrified.

"What's wrong, Jaya?" Alec's breath on her ear gave her a start. She looked up at him and he gave her one of his usual winning smiles. "Isn't that your boy over there?"

She cleared her throat. "Yeah, that's him."

He gave her a gentle nudge. "Then what are you waiting for? You've done all this work to get here." His blue eyes trained on hers. She could read the confusion and worry in them.

She couldn't bear to see him caring about her, so she looked away. It's not like she could tell him that while Brett James might be the guy she was looking for, she was a chicken shit.

Everything she'd ever wanted was finally within her grasp, and she was loitering on the periphery. *Stupid. Stupid. Stupid.*

Alec's earlier words rang through her head over and over again. He'd asked her when she would start looking at her reality. But he'd been right. This life she was so desperate to get back was mostly a fantasy. A fantasy she thought she could live in.

This was reality. She had one job lined up with Adele West-horpe, but she had no others, and no one clamoring to hire her. She actually couldn't get a job in this town, thanks to dear old dad and Derrick. So what choice did she have? She had to pull on her big girl panties. Chugging the rest of her champagne, she strode towards her mark with Alec in tow.

Brett James was in classic Geek Chic. Never mind that it was a rehearsal dinner for a wedding and the attire was cocktail —he wore a Miss Packman T-shirt, with the only concessions to the evening festivities being his dark-wash jeans and his blazer. But from the patches on the tweed jacket, she could tell it was meant to be ironic. On his feet, no loafers for Mr. Tech. Instead, Vans.

Yep, he was one of her people. If she'd gone with her father's pitch, Brett James wouldn't be standing here like he was part of the family. And she'd done that. She'd made it happen. So time to get her job back.

Alec kissed her shoulder. She shivered in delight as she thought of what they'd done before coming to the rehearsal. "Good luck. I'm going to go keep your asshole ex busy so he doesn't interrupt."

She squeezed his hand as he left and drew in a breath. Now or never. She took a step in the right direction, but as her father stepped in her path, she was forced to take two steps back.

"I trust you're enjoying yourself, Jaya."

She rubbed at her nose with a knuckle. "Yeah, fine, Dad." She attempted to peer around his tall frame. "If you'll just excuse me, I need to head to the ladies—"

"Where is that date of yours? Tamara mentioned you were bringing him."

She stiffened. Since when did her father give a shit about her date? "I'm not sure. If you'll just—"

But her father didn't seem to be hearing anything she said. Instead he looked lost in his own train of thought. "If you'll want to continue seeing him, we'll need to have him vetted appropriately, of course. You still have your shares in Trudeaux to protect. Wouldn't want you making the wrong choices. We have to find out what we can about Alec —"

"Aren't you the one who fired me?" She cut him off as her anger brimmed. "Why do you get a say in who I date?" The last thing she needed was a lecture tonight. Especially not a public one. Too bad those were Pierre's specialties. She knew how to perform a preemptive strike.

Her father rolled his eyes. "Don't be so dramatic. You've really been in a snit for much too long."

She sniffed and pulled herself up. "I'm not in a snit. This isn't a toy I want you to go and get from Tamara for me. Though, it's not like you'd actually ever take anything from her."

He shifted to turn his back on her. "If you really must—"

She grabbed his arm and turned him around, not particularly caring if anyone was watching them. She kept her voice low. "You started this line of conversation. Not me." She moved in even closer to him, aware that many of the guests had turned to stare at them now.

"I'm not in a snit. It's not a snit when you expect your father to stand up for and defend you. It's not a snit that I choose not to spend any time with you and/or Tamara and Derrick. I find him to be a vile human being who lied to me, cheated on me, plotted to have me fired, and is now about to marry my sister. Instead of standing up for me and being my dad, you take sides then act like I'm being unreasonable. You fired me from a family business. How the hell am I supposed to feel?"

Pierre brought himself to full height. "This is what I mean, Jaya. You're too emotional. Instead of looking at leaving Trudeaux as an opportunity for new directions, you want to focus on me not taking your side."

Jaya could feel the vein above her eyebrow throbbing, just like his did when he was angry. She stepped back, crossing her arms over her chest. "No. The focus is on the lack of support from you. Not only did you choose a snake-in-the-grass over your own daughter, but you also blocked me from being able to get a job anywhere, deny it, and act like I'm being immature and spiteful."

"You defied a direct order when dealing with the client. That kind of offense is terminable. My actions were just. What would you have done if you were in my shoes? You defy me. You don't listen. You think you know what's best all the time. You don't want to work for a team. You've always worked better on your own. When you don't listen, you get cut from the team. And let me be clear, you are still part of Trudeaux. You have your percentage of the business and the trust fund your mother left you. Do not act like I left you high and dry with nowhere to go."

"Last I checked, my company shares are worthless for voting once Derrick and Tamara marry. I can't ever affect a vote since you have nearly majority shares, and the two of them combined have more shares than I do. So, yeah, I was high and dry with no way to get a job. Though, no thanks to you, I have one now." She shook her head. "Looks like I didn't need you after all." She turned to stalk off and then remembered what he'd said about Alec. "And about my date..." Pierre opened his mouth to speak again, but she held up a hand. "He's been nothing but nice to me, supportive and kind and patient. Your VP Client Services backstabbed me and proposed to my sister and got me fired. And you have no strong words for him?"

"Jaya, I'm merely pointing out that you're keeping company with a man who is, in essence, a drifter. You're not capable of seeing the bad in people, so I have to do it for you."

The flare of temper started to gather energy and she tried to put a muzzle on her murderous thoughts. "You're trying to protect me, are you?"

"Exactly. Whatever you might think, I'm your father, and it's my job to look out for you."

"Then who's going to protect me from you?" She turned on her heel and strode through the hallway into a room full of prying eyes. *Do not cry. Do not cry.* In a hazy fog, all she could focus on was keeping her shoulders back and making her way to the exit on shaky legs. It wasn't until she reached the door that she realized Alec had appeared at her side and held her by the waist.

When they got outside, she wiggled out of his grasp. "Please don't do that."

He frowned. "Do what? I—"

"The whole comforting routine. We've done it before. And you're good at it, but it's not what I need right now. I know it's not real and tonight, that just sucks." She lowered herself on the steps of the Country Club and wrapped her arms around her knees. A migraine loomed behind her left eye socket.

"Jaya." He lowered himself next to her as he loosened his tie. He didn't touch her as he continued. "Maybe right now you don't believe it, but it is real. I do feel something for you, but it doesn't change anything. I'm still leaving. I don't mean to hurt you. Besides, I don't think I'm the one you're mad at right now."

Oh, great. Now the pity. She lifted her chin. "I'm a big girl. I knew this was temporary. It's just when I feel like shit and my stupid father—he knows the buttons to push—well, at times like this I wish it was real. Even though I know better. Even though in a couple of days you'll be gone."

He reached out and wiped a tear from her cheek. "I'm sorry. But I know how this ends up if I stay. I resent you, you learn to hate me, and I have to go."

She narrowed her eyes at him. "If I have to face the truth of where my anger is directed, you have to face the truth of the lies you're telling yourself. You're *choosing* to leave. It's within your power to change that decision." She stood and smoothed out her dress. "I'm going to take a walk. I'll meet you by the car."

EIGHTEEN

Alec didn't know what the hell he was doing here, on Jaya's porch, about to do his best *Say Anything* impression. It would only pique his frustration levels, and that was the last thing he needed. But here he was on her door-step, trying to decide if he should knock or not. What he should have been doing was sitting at home working on Max's return and responding to his latest job offer. Bane's Technology just emailed him with a plum of a job. It was right up his alley—Interim CEO for a two-month stint. In planning for their merger, they'd fired their old CEO and needed someone to drive the whole company towards the merger.

So what was his problem? For starters, he didn't like Jaya factoring in his decision. Second, it was killing him that he hadn't been able to stop thinking about her since the other night at the rehearsal. Worse than that, she hadn't called. The way she'd looked so vulnerable had nearly broken his heart. And he only had two more days before the board of directors would call the authorities and Max would officially be a wanted man. Alec actually had shit to do if he was going to keep it all afloat.

But instead of focusing on what was important, he was here, on her doorstep. Maybe she was right about him. He'd always told Mimi he couldn't be tied down, but the truth was he'd never tried to stay. He'd obeyed Mimi's rules and stuck around until he went to college, but the moment he had no obligations, he'd been off. Maybe he was just running away like Max did. Maybe he was no different.

He shook his head. No. He was different, he told himself. He never hurt anybody. Except Mimi. Except Jaya.

As he paced a raw patch in Jaya's welcome mat, he had a good idea about what was niggling at his brain. He'd known Jaya for less than two weeks and he was already sprung like a school kid with his first crush. He'd been unable to get any of his work done. He'd sat in for Max on the Board of Director's meeting, but fat lot of good that did. They wanted to speak to Max. And good for Adele. She hadn't protected his brother. She'd been clear and concise about Max's culpability. But now he only had another two days to find his brother, or there would be police involvement.

He ran his hands through his hair. What was wrong with him? He couldn't focus on his family or on his future prospects. He should have already replied to the Bane's Technology job. It was a no-brainer. The money was great—kind of obscene, actually. And it would give him freedom for at least another six months if he wanted to make the trek through Africa happen.

Only problem was, it was in Boston. Three thousand freaking miles away from Jaya. His brain had already pushed his emotional centers toward rationality, worked all the rational scenarios. He'd only known Jaya for a couple of weeks. It was supposed to be all about sex. Exceptionally hot sex that he would consider cutting his own arm off to have again, but it wasn't like he was in love with her. She and her damn lists. So stubborn. None of those arguments mattered, because here he was, acting like a moron. Pacing. And pissed off at himself for needing her.

Damn it. Make up your mind, man. He either needed to knock or get the fuck out of here because the neighbors probably thought he was stalkerazzi.

He lifted his hand to knock but didn't manage it before she opened the door. As soon as she saw him, her eyes widened and his name came out in a soft breath. It was all he could do to keep his inward groan silent, but something inside him roared. He wanted her. And it wasn't just the sex. Though he knew he'd die if he didn't feel her against him again. But he just needed her. He wanted someone to talk to, to laugh with. *Fuck.* He sounded like a sap.

It took him several moments to realize she was speaking. "Alec. Earth to Alec. What are you doing here? I thought you were working today?" She waved a hand in front of his face. In her other hand she held a bag of cans. Probably headed for the recycling bin down the hall. He tried to speak, but no words came forth. After all what could he say? Instead, he moved.

Grabbing her hand he pulled her back through her door. She had on a white sundress with butterflies and simple white canvas slip-on shoes. She tried tugging her hand free, but he held fast.

"Alec, what the hell are you doing?"

He didn't answer her and ignored the litter of cans in her foyer, tugging her through her living room to the balcony. Could he tell her how he felt?

Jaya wiggled and squirmed in his grasp. "Alec, you can't just show up and not say anything and then drag me around. You don't have to do the Conan the Barbarian routine. Or at least if we're going to play Conan, let me get the right outfit for this adventure."

Shit. She was right. He was acting like a total ass. He also tried not to picture her in some scrap of rawhide leather, pretending to be Conan's conquest. Granted, this was more of the real him than he ever showed.

Pausing, he drew in a deep breath, unaccustomed to giving apologies.

"I'm sorry about the other night. You were right. I am choosing to leave. But I'm telling you the truth when I tell you that you make me think about staying."

She winced. "I'm sorry about that. I was totally raw from my conversation with Dad. Here's the thing. We had an arrangement. You should want to stay because of you, not because of me."

A smile tugged at his lips. He did like direct women. "It's more than that. I—" Shit, what was he doing? Apologizing for who he was? "I..." His voice trailed off. He tried again. *I'm afraid of how much I need you.* "We have two days. I—" He couldn't finish the thought.

"Are you sure you're all right?"

Alec shook his head and shoved his hands in his pockets. "Yeah, I'm good. I just needed to see you. And say I'm sorry." If that wasn't the understatement of the century. "And I'm sorry for barging in like this."

She held her arms out to the sides. "You're seeing me."

Damn, she really wasn't giving him any rope. *Well, here I go then.* "I missed you. And I've been pretty useless the last couple of days. No one's offered to make me a list to get my life in order in over forty-eight hours. I've been missing it."

She grinned. "I do make an excellent project plan. Especially now that I have my software."

Just the mere mention of the software reminded him of how they'd retrieved it. His cock bulged behind his jeans. Clearing his throat, he spoke. "Do you trust me?"

Her eyes narrowed instantly. "Define 'trust.'"

And there it was. The underlying reason why being anywhere near her was a challenge. "Do you trust me to not do anything to hurt you?"

This time she just cocked her head and folded her arms over her chest.

Okay. She had a point. "Let me amend that. Do you trust me to help you with your list? I had an idea of how to cross something else off."

He noticed the pink flush on her cheek bones. The moment she gave him her slow nod, he continued tugging her to the balcony. As soon as she realized where they were headed, she tried to release her hand. "I don't know what you have planned, but have you forgotten the balcony is completely exposed to the doorman's office?"

He let his smile speak for him. The look on her face as dawning hit was priceless. Her lips formed a small "O" and her cheeks went pink again. His own skin felt tight. He needed to be with her. He didn't care where. Floor, bed, couch. Didn't matter to him. Most of him would prefer no one watch them. But he wasn't here for himself. He wanted to fulfill a fantasy of hers. Something to cross off her list. And if he was good for nothing else, he was her personal adventurist.

Pulling her to him, he kissed her long and deep pouring out every emotion into her. He tried pulling her through the doorway to the balcony, but her feet rooted to the floor.

"What's wrong?" He searched her face for some clue that he'd done something wrong.

"I didn't say I didn't want to go on the balcony. I just need to psych myself up."

Nodding solemnly, he bent and traced kisses along her jaw. "Allow me to help." Opening the sliding glass door, he tugged her through onto the balcony. Under the awning, there was a perfunctory patio table with two chairs and the canvas bench he'd noticed the last time he was here.

Carrying her to the ledge nearest the doormen's office, he gently placed her down, giving her drugging kisses designed to make her forget her name and where she was. When she moaned against his lips and dug her fingers in his hair, he forgot all about who may or may not be watching. All he knew was that he already loved her. And it terrified him.

JAYA COULDN'T BELIEVE what they were doing. She'd been miserable the past few days. Then here he was, about to take her to a fantasy place. The kind of place that people might never get to go. And he was offering it to her on a plate. Or balcony, as the case may be. The breeze blew and she shivered, though not from any cold in the air.

He separated her thighs and stepped between her legs. His lips coaxed a response from hers, nipping and nibbling, exploring and tasting. Alec knew how to kiss. Amongst other things. Her head fogged as the pleasure coursed through her. Senses heightened, Jaya could feel every sensitized patch of flesh as Alec ran his fingers over her upper thighs.

He lifted his lips from hers and she blinked up at his heavy-lidded gaze. "You can turn back at any time, okay? Any time you feel uncomfortable, just tell me. I only want to take care of you."

She nodded, unable to form any words. What if she couldn't go through with this? What if she'd taken a hot fantasy and screwed it up by trying to accomplish it? What if—

The corner of his lips tipped up in a lopsided smile. "And no worrying about failure if you want to stop. This is supposed to be fun. No lists. Just feel. Be happy."

The words were soft and lulled her. The slow circles he drew with his thumb on her thighs sent shivers of excitement through her body as they moved closer and closer to her panty line. As his thumbs snuck under the elastic of the lace fabric, they both groaned. She, because she finally had the contact she'd been craving, and he, likely because he'd found her little surprise.

He smoothed his thumb over her slick folds. "When did you do this?" His voice was rough and disoriented.

She shifted in his grasp, trying to get closer. "The day of the rehearsal dinner. I wanted to surprise you."

He dropped his head to hers as his thumbs kept up the stroking of her smooth slit to her hyper-sensitive clit. "If I wished I wasn't such an idiot before. This seals it."

She ran her teeth over his earlobe and he swore softly. "You're here now. Want to do something about the surprise?"

His soft laugh didn't surprise her. This was more the Alec she knew. Not as intense. But the new Alec was hotter, more focused. More determined. As he took her lips again, he shoved down the straps of her dress exposing one of her breasts to his view. She tried to wiggle out of the straps, but he held her tight.

"Not yet. I'll have you naked soon enough." He bent his

head to suckle her, taking greedy pulls of her nipple. He used his finger to enter her as his thumb continued to stroke her clit.

Unable to think, unable to breathe, all Jaya could do was throw her head back in ecstasy. "Yes, Alec." She knew what was coming for her. She'd come to crave it. Had been unable to sleep without having him sink into her and give her one of those soul-shattering orgasms. As Alec stroked her tight pussy, she could feel his urgency, his intensity. He wanted her to come. And she was more than ready to comply.

But as she felt the little quakes start deep in her core, Alec slowed the pace of his penetrating finger, then stopped stroking her clit all together. Confused, she looked up at him.

"I know, sweetheart." He chuckled. "You were so close. But I don't want you to come without knowing someone else wants you almost as much as I do."

Whipping her head around, she looked into the window of the doormen's office to find Marco leaning intently against the window frame. His dark eyes pinned on her and Alec. She could see the intensity in his dark eyes, the need there. It made her hot all over. Even hotter as Alec resumed his ministrations with his fingers and mumbled against her neck, "Do you see what you're doing to him? Do you see how much he wants you?"

She nodded, and Alec pinched her clit. Surprised at the stinging pleasure-pain, she focused her attention back on him.

"I want to hear you. I want Marco to hear you." He nuzzled her ear. "One more time. Do you see what you're doing to him? Do you like him watching you?"

She licked her lips in a vain attempt to bring moisture back to them. "Y-Yes."

"Can you feel how much I want you?" He drew her hand to his straining cock behind the zipper of his jeans.

She smiled. This was familiar territory. "Yes. Maybe I should help you with that."

"You should definitely help me with this, but I want your attention, your focus on Marco. I want you to watch him as he watches you. Do you understand?"

She nodded, and then amended her answer with a soft. "Yes, Alec." Turning her attention back to Marco, she watched as the sexy Brazilian smiled and winked at her. She focused on how Alec was making her feel, how it felt to know Marco was watching her.

Alec hooked his thumbs into her panties, pulling them down her thighs off her feet. When he lowered himself between her legs, she moaned. His tongue, sure and agile, stroked her silken core, teased her clit, and took no prisoners. He made a small humming noise as his lips circled the delicate button and pleasure washed over her. She had no choice but to watch Marco as she wound her hands in Alec's hair. Her orgasm was quick and came without warning. On a breath, all she could do was moan out, "Alec."

He was smiling as he came back up her body, placing feathery kisses along the way. "You are so unbelievably beautiful. Do you know that?"

She flushed. She'd never get used to his effusive praising. Especially not in bed. He was completely unselfish and just wanted to give her pleasure.

"Are you okay?"

She melted against him. "Yes. Better than all right." Lifting her head up, she looked into his eyes. "But I miss you. I want you."

"Don't worry, we're getting to that." Smoothing his hands over her thighs, he gathered up the fabric of her dress and brought it over her head. As soon as the dress was on the ground, he kissed her long and deep, with intent to brand. Intended to let her know who she was fucking. She tried to help him with his belt and jeans, but he brushed her hands away. "Baby, if you touch me, I'm not going to last very long. A guy's got to have his pride."

Oh right, they weren't alone. "We can go back inside," she said as he hurriedly shed his clothes. "You gave me my fantasy."

Naked, in all his masculine beauty, he studied her. "Are you enjoying yourself?"

She nodded a response. "What do you think?"

"Does it make you uncomfortable?"

She glanced back at Marco, who was slowly stroking himself through his jeans. She knew the right answer was that she was bothered, but the truth was, she wasn't. It still didn't feel real. Yes it was Marco. And she knew him, but he was leaving and she wouldn't have to see him again, so nothing awkward or uncomfortable. "No, it makes me feel sexy and desired."

His smile was tight. "And you are. I'm aching for you." The blunt head of his cock nudged her entrance and he cursed.

When Alec entered her, filling her to the hilt, she held onto him tight. She would never get used to how he made her feel. As he held her on the railing, he stroked her nice and slow, rubbing her nipples with his thumbs as if they had all the time in the world. With every stroke, she shivered as the ridge of his cock head reached her G-spot.

"Yes, Alec. Right there."

"Damn, baby, you're so tight. I could stay here forever."

She wrapped her legs around him, lifting her chest to give

him better access to her breast. He rewarded her by licking first the left nipple then the right, circling each tip with his sure tongue, drawing a response from her, bringing her closer and closer to another peak. The intimacy rocked her. Desperate to hide from him, from herself, Jaya turned her attention to Marco.

But instead of lessening the intimacy between them, looking at Marco only increased the connection to Alec. She watched, transfixed, as Marco released his magnificent cock from his jeans. He wasn't as thick as Alec was, but he was a little longer, the skin of his penis darker than his bronzed skin. As he worked his hand over the cock, Jaya could see the drop of moisture oozing out of the tip.

Alec grunted as he slid into her again and again, branding her as his. "Do you want him close enough to touch Jaya? Do you want to feel his hands on you? Do you want to have your ultimate fantasy fulfilled"

Her skin, already so heated from his caress and his lips, burned. Was this wrong? Did she really want this? Could she have sex with Alec and Marco? Could she have Marco's hands on her body even as Alec loved her? She hesitated. She'd wanted this fantasy, but now that she was here, could she go through with it? Was this about the fantasy or was this about wanting to hide from a level of intimacy with Alec. "No. All I want is you."

"Are you sure?"

As she nodded slowly, she met Alec's gaze. From some of their late night pillow talks, she knew he had threesomes before. Maybe with other men? Maybe this was nothing to him. "Being with you is hotter than any random fantasy I had once. This is actually real."

Alec exhaled a long breath. His eyes burned as he spoke to

Marco. "You can only watch. I'm the *only* one who gets to touch her."

Jaya shivered at the fierce conviction in his voice. Alec responded to the change in her. His thrusts were no longer measured, but more frenzied, more eager as if staking a claim, marking her as his forever.

Alec her long and deep while he played with her breasts. He broke the kiss and whispered harshly into her ear. "Remember who's inside you. Remember who knows how to make you feel good. Remember, I know what you like."

Alec pinched her nipple and her body quaked. He circled her clit with his thumb and her body rocked into another orgasm she thought would tear her apart.

But he didn't let her catch her breath, just gritted his teeth over her orgasm and continued to penetrate her with deep strokes.

Alec tipped her torso closer to him so she fell farther onto his cock. "I know what you like, Jaya. Do you want to show your new friend?" She tensed, but he hushed her. "I won't let anything happen to you."

She was so boneless, she just relaxed against him. Turning her head to look at Marco, she saw his attention was on Alec's hand as his finger delved between her ass cheeks to find the bundle of nerves she loved to have stroked. As Alec penetrated with a finger, she held still. He whispered to her, "It's okay—you can get used to the feeling."

The look in Marco's eyes was one of untold lust, but he stroked himself in lazy motions. Alec removed his finger and she whimpered. "It's okay baby, I just need to hold you tighter so we don't topple over."

As Alec held her hips still, his strokes picked up the pace

again. Teeth gritted, he looked like he was concentrating on not coming, like he was holding something back from her. She frowned. This was not her Alec. But before she could focus too hard, he took possession of her nipple while his deft fingers found the pocket of nerves at her rear again. Raw pleasure speared and rippled through her and she broke apart again in his arms.

Through her haze of ecstasy-filled orgasm, she barely registered it when Alec ground out a string of unrecognizable words as his release heated her from the inside. Jaya could feel his release deep inside her and she stared at him in wonder. Behind her she heard Marco moan his own release. Her body melted in Alec's embrace.

Minutes later, after Marco closed the office window and Jaya caught her breath, Alec drew her a bath. He was so gentle with her she could have wept. No one had ever taken care of her like that. When he gently washed her skin and massaged each of her sore muscles, she wondered how she'd survive it when he left her behind.

NINETEEN

Alec felt like an ass. A well-sated ass, but an ass nonetheless. An ass who had broken his own rule and fallen hard for an uptight, hyper-planning, gorgeous woman who he'd hurt when he left. She shifted in his arms and he tightened his grip on her. "Where do you think you're going?"

She wiggled again. "I need to finish cleaning up, figure out what I'm wearing to the wedding on Saturday. Prep the cards of "Who's Who" for the wedding. I can't just laze in bed all day."

He smiled into her hair and the smell of roses wafted into his nostrils. So it was her shampoo that drove him wild. Good to know. He'd buy her a case of it. With his luck, he'd never be able to smell the stuff again without thinking about her. "Yes, you can. When was the last time you slept in past seven in the morning?"

She remained silent.

"It's not a trick question, you know."

"No. I know. I'm just thinking."

He chuckled. "You're always up with the birds, huh?"

Giggling she nodded. "Mom used to try and get me to stay

in bed. When I was a kid, she'd entice me and Tamara with wrapped sausages in bed if we pretended we were camping. Somehow, I still never made it past eight."

"But it's not morning, is it." He kissed her shoulder.

"You do have a point." He felt some of the tension leave his body as she pressed into him. Her body, the perfect mold for his. His arms tightened again, and he knew he'd have a hell of a time leaving. Temporary or not, his heart was already gone.

He finally took stock of her bedroom layout. It looked like a nod to a contemporary hotel. Everything had its place. Nothing strewn about. She hadn't even known he was coming but her whole place was this pin neat? How could she live like this? He was sure he'd left his underwear right where he'd dropped them in the living room. The one exception to the almost obsessive compulsive neatness was an accent wall. There were five strips of brightly colored paint. "What's with the wall?" She wiggled again, but he held tighter.

She shifted in his arms. "When I moved in here, I thought it might be a good idea to add a little pop of color to things, but every color was a little too much."

"What was wrong with the red?"

She shook her head. "It was too brick. It looked really dark and sort of made me feel like the room looked like a bordello.

He chuckled. "So what you mean to tell me is the red was too red."

She smacked his arm. "Not exactly, but I didn't see myself as really a red person."

"Okay, so what was wrong with the teal? Too blue?"

"Shut up. It was a little more aquamarine that it looked in the store. Sort of made me seasick."

"And the lavender, well, I can see why you didn't pick that

one. It even makes me want to puke. But what's wrong with the yellow? I think it's nice and cheery."

She rolled her eyes. "Whatever. I didn't like it." She wrapped one of the sheets around herself and made to get up. He reached for her.

"Oh, come on, I was only teasing you. Maybe color isn't your thing. Not everyone has to be Rainbow Bright."

She sighed and sat on the edge of the bed. "My mom loved color. Every year, she gave me some article of clothing that was so bright it hurt my eyes. Dad always said the bright colors made me look like a tart."

"Is that where all this comes from? Your father, who's obviously got a stick up his—" She cast him a look and he tried a different tactic. "Okay. What about your clothes? I've never seen you in anything but black and white and gray. Well, there was that one red dress you wore to the club that night. Very hot, by the way."

"Very hot equals Micha. I don't think she owns a single neutral color." She sighed. "Sometimes I wish I could wave a magic wand and it would be done with the perfect color. I don't want to choose wrong."

He shook his head. "I don't really think it's a 'right or wrong' kind of thing. What are you wearing Saturday?"

Jaya wrapped the blanket even tighter around herself. "What, you're my stylist now?"

"No, but I know what I like. And I have a good idea what might look really good on you."

Since he met her, he pictured her in the gold color of those shoes she loved so much. "Come on, we'll get in the shower and go shopping. Find you something to wear that will make your father nuts."

Bingo. That got a sly smile on her face.

"I would love to, but I can't. Those damn shoes have cost me more than my budget will allow. You forget, I don't have a permanent job now."

Damn, leave it to her to be practical. "You *do* have a job, remember? Besides, I know the best place. And the dress won't cost you a thing. The owner owes me a favor. So you can have a borrowed dress." Adele probably wouldn't approve, but at this point, it wasn't like he was using his brain. He just wanted to see her happy.

"A borrowed dress. Who are all these people who owe you favors?" She held up a hand. "Never mind. I have a sneaking suspicion I don't want to know."

"One caveat—you have to let me pick the dress."

She stood and the blanket pooled at her feet. "I get veto power."

He shook his head. "Nope."

"But I have to. It has to be tasteful enough for the wedding. I can't run around in something short and cleavage-bearing."

Alec propped his head up against the pillows. "What if I love your cleavage?" *What if I love you?* But he wisely kept that last part to himself, as if by not voicing it, it didn't exist.

She blushed. "You really are incorrigible. It's a wedding. An evening one, but still. I'm not going to pull a Pippa Middleton and wear white to my sister's wedding. Or red, either."

With a look of mock shock, he clutched his hand over his heart. "You wound me. You act like I have no taste."

"Are you going to let it go?"

He shook his head. "Do I look like the kind of guy to let it go?"

Jaya flopped back on the bed, clutching the sheet to her breasts. "Fine, you can borrow me a dress."

Two hours after he returned from his shopping trip with Jaya, he and Caleb prepared her surprise. He sent a silent prayer to all the gods he could think of that she loved it.

"Alec, why is it every time you say you need my help with something it involves manual labor?" Caleb wielded the paint roller, splashing Royal Gold onto Jaya's bedroom wall.

With any luck, he and Caleb would get it done in a couple of hours. Of course, tonight, he and Jaya would have to sleep at his place because of the fumes, but he didn't think she'd mind. She talked so much about how she'd loved the color of his suite, he'd asked housekeeping what it was. He was as nervous as a school kid about her reaction.

"What can I say? You're a sucker for a friend."

"Said friend needs to tell me what he wants from now on. Give a guy a chance to make informed decisions."

"Quit your bitchin'. Where are we with Max? I need to leave in a couple of days if I'm going to make that race."

Caleb shook his head as he maneuvered the edger around the top corner wall. "I talked to my buddy at the FBI. We might be able to get him some kind of deal if he comes clean with any information he has about the Sandovals. They'll also let him keep any money he has left from his trust fund. And he'll get witness protection, but he'll have to testify."

Alec nodded. "I underestimated his ball size. Pretty sure little brother has a death wish. Not to mention, the moron gene runs through his DNA. Pisses me off that he ran out on Adele."

Caleb's non-committal "Mm-hmm" had Alec flashing him an irritated glance.

"You're worse than a chick. What's with the sanctimonious?"

His friend snorted. "Look, all I'm saying is you're being really hard on him. I barely like the guy—he's put Adele in danger—but it's not like you haven't made any mistakes. And it's also not like you haven't bailed a couple of times yourself."

Ah, so that was it.

"Let me ask you something, Alec. What's the longest you've held a job?"

That was easy. "Five years. I've had my business for five years."

"You're cheating with semantics. But whatever. Let's take your contracts. What's the longest any of those contracts have lasted?"

Alec didn't like where this was going. "Six months."

"And of the ones lasting over three months, how many have you terminated prematurely because of creative differences?"

Alec clamped his lips shut. He had a reputation for being the best. But he also had a reputation for not putting up with bullshit. If things weren't done his way, he severed the contract.

"Cat got your tongue, buddy? Okay, how about relationships. After Adele, what's the longest relationship with a woman you've had? Shoot, you barely even keep them as friends."

"I have relationships." Though he struggled to think of one that truly mattered. Caleb chuckled without humor. "Yeah, if by relationships you mean a string of one-night stands. Or two-week stands, as is the case now."

Alec wielded his paint brush like a weapon. "You got a point?"

"Just that we all have shit we're running from. You being mad at Max 'cause he ran is really about you being mad at yourself. Your brother, we'll find him. And you'll bring him home. Just like you always do." In a softer voice, Caleb added, "And yeah, you're going to leave, but there's a difference between the two of you. When it counts, you're always there, no questions. But you can't be so cut and dry with him. It certainly won't help bring him home."

"Okay, Oprah, I hear you. But I—" The sound of the front door slamming had him calling out. "Jai, is that you?" Lord knew how many others had keys to this place. Her sister, her friends.

The sound of her voice got louder as she got closer to the bedroom. "Alec? You're still here? Why does it smell like wet pai—" Abruptly she stopped talking as she stood in the doorway and stared.

Her look of shock was priceless. "Surprise." He spread his arms wide. "You remember Caleb? Well I enlisted his help in getting you that pop of color you've been looking for."

Her eyes darted from Alec, to Caleb, then back to Alec. She opened her mouth to speak, but nothing came out and she closed her mouth again. Flattening her full lips. She tried again, succeeding this time. "Caleb, thank you for helping to paint my bedroom, but could you give me a minute with Alec?"

"Sure thing." He made haste getting out of there and threw Alec an *I'm sorry buddy* glance. As soon as the door closed, Jaya turned her attention to him.

"What the hell do you think you're doing?"

Not what he expected "Okay, you don't look happy, but really, I was only trying to help." He dropped the paint brush into the tray and shoved his hands in his jeans.

"Help? What made you think you were helping me? I'll have to get a paint crew in here to undo it all."

"Oh, c'mon. Why the hell would you do that? I did something nice."

She surveyed her room. "By doing something that was more about your satisfaction than mine? I never asked you to do this. Shit, I didn't even pick the color."

"It's the same color as my suite at the hotel. You always say you like it. And left to you, you never would have made a decision on the color."

"So you push me into a decision? That's bullshit, Alec. I didn't want this. I didn't get to make the choice for myself. And that's kind of the point."

Fuck, he'd gotten it wrong. He shrugged. "It's only paint." He shook his head. "I guess I didn't think it through."

"No. You didn't. You got all caught up in the adventure of it. Just like you always do. Now I have to find the funds to hire painters to undo it all."

Anger simmered in his blood. She would undo the paint, just like she would erase him from her life when he was gone. She'd been clear she wasn't able to trust, and he'd been clear he was not into sticking around. Except he'd gone and changed his mind. "I'll pay for the painters."

Her chuckle held no humor. "Oh really? You're on a bartender-slash-Guy Friday salary. How are you going to manage that? Like you pointed out this morning, I have a job again, so as soon as I'm clear of the shoe credit-card monster I'll take care of it." She sniffed. "And I'll need to go stay at Micha's or Ricca's."

And she wasn't going to stay with him. *Fantastic.* His day was certainly looking up. Well, at least he'd accepted the job. Until now it had felt like a mistake. But maybe it was the right move after all.

TWENTY

Jaya's annoyance poured over her like a mudslide down a mountain. "Stupid asshole painted my bedroom."

Micha and Ricca exchanged looks. Ricca spoke up. "Okay. So weren't you just saying you'd been trying to paint the place for two years and could never decide? So maybe he thought he was doing you a favor." She shrugged. "I mean, it was kind of sweet."

Micha gave a little shake of her head as if warning her that the cobra would strike at any moment.

Jaya was in no mood to hear clear rational arguments.

"So you're fine with Charles just marching in and changing everything about your life. Taking it over?"

Ricca's frown was tight. "No, but is that really what—"

Jaya didn't pay any attention to her friend's attempts at reason. "He just barged into my life, with his sexy smile and hair to die for, and started changing everything. If he didn't like me and my white walls the way they were, what the hell is he doing painting them? You can't just change something you don't like about someone. You have to learn to love it."

Micha unfolded her long legs from the floor cushion and stood. "Okay, look. Maybe you're right. He shouldn't try and change you, but how is it changing you if you told him your dream was to have someone magically come in and make the changes for you? So you didn't have to do any of the work of painting, let alone picking a color. He was trying to be helpful."

Jaya scowled at her friends. "You're taking his side."

Micha quirked a brow. "Before you go all, 'Alec has pulled them over to the dark side on me,' might I remind you that *you* were the one who decided to approach a random stranger and then have sex with him. Even though all you talk about half the time are crazed serial killers."

"Yes, but—"

"Aren't you the one who convinced this poor man into helping you break into your old place of employment to go and take software that is technically yours?"

"Yes, but—"

"Did he force you to do any of these things?"

"No."

"Then why are you mad at him?"

Having run out of steam, Jaya leaned against the cushions. "I sort of liked guessing which color. I really wanted to pick it out myself."

Micha rolled her eyes. "Newsflash, you're being a bitch. And a bratty one at that. You can do anything you want to the whole living room. He tried to do something special for you. And instead of being with him and giving him all kinds of raunchy thank you sex, you're sitting around my living room full of piss and vinegar."

"What's really upsetting you, sweetie?" Ricca asked.

Jaya blew out a breath. "Not being in control. He just took it out of my hands and it sucks."

Micha leaned forward. "Now, for that he's an asshole—a sweet asshole, but he shouldn't have taken control from you. You want me to straighten him out?" She waggled her eyebrows. "Could be fun."

Jaya leaned back in her seat, deflated. They were right. She was being a snotty brat. He'd done something sweet and she'd let her temper rip him a new one. Stupid. "Anyone have any ideas on what a really big apology looks like?"

ALEC LOOKED up from the bar to see Jaya striding into Synthesis. A small smile hit his lips. That was Jaya. No guile. No sashaying, not strutting, just straight to the point, get to business. He liked that about her.

As she walked toward him, she waved a little white handkerchief and smiled sheepishly. He knew she was here to apologize. And the weight he'd been carrying around since their fight lifted. But his more practical side understood that it would be easier if she'd stayed mad at him and hadn't seen him again. But easier for who? Why did he put his hands on something that he knew he couldn't have? "Because I'm a masochist that's why," he mumbled under his breath.

"What did you say?" she asked as she grabbed a bar stool and plopped a folder and her handkerchief on the counter.

"Nothing." He smiled. "You look dressed for an interview. Are you already giving up on Adele?"

She glanced down at her outfit. Brow furrowed, she asked, "What's wrong with what I'm wearing?"

The light gray pin stripe suit was form fitting and cut to fit her slender curves. And she was wearing those mouthwatering shoes again. All he could think about was her wearing nothing but those shoes as they wrapped around his back and she screamed his name. He cleared his throat in an effort to clear the imagery. "Not a thing."

She shrugged. "I just finished with Adele. Besides, Tamara called and wanted some help at the wedding site, so I'll go by for an hour. Best to have my armor on."

Ah, so that was it. "You want to drive her crazy with curiosity as to who you're working for?"

She shrugged. "A little. Petty maybe, but not even close to what she's pulled."

"Good point." He reached out and touched her hand. The usual rush of emotion and need didn't surprise him this time. But it did make him want to do things to her in the bar that probably weren't legal in fifteen states. "About yesterday—"

She put up a hand and interrupted him. "No. Please let me." She shook her head. "I was a total brat and ungrateful. I realize you were only trying to be nice. Clearly, I have a hard time with relinquishing control."

Alec folded his arms instead, in the hope he'd keep them to himself. He really wanted to hold her. It had only been a week and a half since they'd started seeing each other, but it was already an automatic thing. "I should have asked you. I don't ask very often. I just 'do'. Sometimes it backfires. I can paint it back the way you had it."

The smile she gave him half melted his heart. "No. Please don't. I kind of like it. Something for me to remember you by when you leave."

Ouch. He winced. That ugly little detail. He would be

leaving her in no time. "Next time I'll ask first," he promised solemnly, but they both knew that there wouldn't be a next time. "I've started to like your bossy Type-A style."

She dipped her head and changed the subject. "So, Mr. Bartender, you feel like giving me a lesson?"

He wasn't sure he heard her correctly. "Exactly what kind of lesson were you looking for?" His libido started to fantasize.

"It's something on my Thirty list. I had this ridiculous notion after college that I'd find myself and tend bar or something like that to pay the rent. Either that or strip." She shook her head. "Stupid, right? I was kidding about the stripping part, by the way."

"Too bad. And no. I'd buy a drink from you any day."

She grinned at him. "So, how about a lesson?"

His brows drew in. "What? Right now?"

She slipped off her jacket. "Yeah, what's wrong with now?"

Maybe because he was on edge, because he could still smell her roses shampoo and it was driving him nuts.

She slid back behind the bar with him. "Show me how to make what you gave me the other night. I don't know what was in that, but it was delicious."

She brushed against him just enough to have him reciting his favorite childhood baseball players. "Um, that one's pretty easy." Bending down, he took the ingredients from the fridges under the bar. Setting down the cranberry, orange and pineapple juices, he got a glass and handed it to her. "First, rim the glass." He winced at the obvious sexual reference. It conjured up all kinds of imagery of the two of them.

She took it from him, her delicate fingers barely brushing his in the transfer. She dipped the glass in the sugar tray.

He placed his hand on hers. "Like this. You'll want to rim the glass with lemon first. It'll help the sugar stick to the glass."

She did as he told her, then grinned up at him. "What next?"

"Now add one part pineapple and one part orange juice."

She used the little measuring cup and he didn't have the heart to tell her no real bartender worth his or her salt would measure the amount of juice that went into a drink. The alcohol, maybe, if trying to save the bar some cash. But not juice. But she liked things to be precise and that's why he liked her. "Done. What next."

The way her smile caught the light, Alec knew he was in trouble. If by chance he made it through the next day or so, his fate would be changed forever. He loved her. It was that simple. He didn't give a shit about consequences. All he knew was that he wanted her. Lists and all. Clearing his throat, he pulled down a bottle of Grand Marnier. "Add a splash of this."

She frowned. The bottle hovered just over the mixer.

"What's the matter?"

She chewed her lip. "How much is a splash? More than the juice or less than the juice? Is it a big splash? Can I just measure it, instead?"

He took the bottle from her and set it on the counter. "It doesn't have to be perfect, you know. It's just a drink."

She nodded, but he could see the telltale shimmer in her eyes. "Just a drink," she mumbled.

He shrugged. "Or maybe it's the epitome of your whole life, and your entire existence hinges on getting this drink just right." He took her hands. "But I promise you. It doesn't." Her lips quirked. He continued, "Everything doesn't have to be perfect.

You don't have to be perfect. But newsflash, you're already pretty perfect to me."

"Lists and all?"

He flashed her a grin. "Lists and all. Go on, add as much Grand Marnier as you want." She poured enough to give any drinker a kick.

Handing her the shaker, he said, "Now shake it up and pour."

As she poured, he tried not to watch her delicate fingers and wonder where they'd be better served. He had to get a grip.

She handed him the glass. "Did I get it right?"

He didn't take a sip.

"You taste it and tell me."

Her lips parted and his whole body jerked. As the blissful expression crossed her face as she sipped, he smiled. "Good?"

She nodded. "Yeah, tastes just like it."

"You're now officially a bartender. You can cross that off your Thirty list."

Eyeing the go-go dance platforms next to the booths, she smiled. "I have something better to cross off the list."

♛

USING the back of the booth as balance, Jaya climbed up onto the table. "I've always wanted to do this. You got any music for me?"

His gaze burned into hers before going over to the laptop plugged into the sound system. The nerves took hold of her stomach. She didn't have to prove anything to him. But she did have to prove it to herself. She wasn't that woman who was so scared to fail, who never took any chances. Shit, the biggest chance she'd ever taken was with that presentation, and look where it had gotten her.

A brand new job with a woman who could make her career and a fling with a man hot enough to leave scorch marks on her bed. As chances went, she picked a hell of a chance to take. Her family might be a mess, but maybe it was time to leave Trudeaux anyway. Though, she'd have preferred to do it on her terms.

She could do this. Alec was safe. Considering everything they'd already experienced and shared, she knew she was safe.

The jazzy intro of the song had her smiling. En Vogue—"*Giving Him Something He Can Feel.*" Well, she'd do that, all right. She slipped the stilettos off and set them aside. Maybe she could make them work for her later. Unpinning her hair, she tousled it. Alec watched her from the bar, but he still didn't say anything or come near her.

As the voices of the En Vogue girls filled the club, she closed her eyes and felt the music, letting the rhythm guide her hips.

His response? Cocking his head.

Fair enough—she could do better than that. She steadied herself on the pole with one hand while the other tousled her hair as En Vogue continued to sing about how a man's love would send them on and on. Pausing at the opening of her blouse she popped one button, then the others in quick succession. Turning her attention to Alec, she realized he'd stopped drying glasses.

As she rolled her hips in time to the jazz saxophone, she pictured Alec's hands on her, turning her hips and bracing her hands on the pole. She imagined having him direct her movements and complied. She danced for both of them.

Stroking her hands down her torso, she undid the loop of

her pants and let them slide down to the booth exposing her garters and lack of underwear.

From the bar, all she heard was, "Sweet Jesus." But it was faint as the chorus went on about giving him something he can feel. In time to the music, she turned to face Alec. Touching herself with both hands, pausing to pinch her nipples through the fabric of her bra. Undoing the front clasp, she let them hang full and free. But she didn't pause to enjoy the pleasured pain, the pinching shot to her core. She let her hands skim over her belly, watching Alec through lowered lashes.

He leaned on the bar, eyes intent. Heat and passion burning in his stare. The need for her apparent in his heavy lidded gaze. Was he thinking about the way Marco had watched them on her balcony?

In the mood to tease, she let her fingers skim over the lips of her pussy. Between the folds, seeking—Ahh. As the tips of her fingers came into contact with her wet heat, she moaned and tossed her head back.

When she opened her eyes again, Alec was standing right in front of her. Clearing his throat, he asked, "Can I get a private lap dance?"

She gave him a slow nod and he lifted her off the table, letting her slide down his form. The farther she slid, the more she realized he'd been touching himself. And that his cock was free from the confines of his jeans. "Alec."

The kiss he planted on her was all raw heat and lust. The need for her was obvious, she could feel him throbbing. He pulled them down onto the booth and she turned to face away from him, giving him a view of her ass.

"God, that's a thing of beauty."

As she danced, his hands roamed over her back and her breasts, dug into the flesh of her ass.

Standing to join her, his hips kept time with hers as they danced. "Do you know what you're doing to me?" The tone of his voice was so low, it was barely a growl.

"Just returning the favor." Who was this new woman who held her own with someone like Alec?

He leaned her against the table and steadied her. "Hold on tight."

He fiddled with his wallet for several seconds.

In the distance, she heard the foil tearing.

The head of his thick, throbbing cock met the well of her core and he swore. Jaya knew how wet she was, knew she was ready for him. He didn't need to take his time—this was what she wanted, what she needed. He slid into her to the hilt and roared.

The pleasure built up in her spine with each thrust. With each forward movement of his hips, he called her name. Loudly. Reverently. With one hand, he steadied her hips even as he slid in easily. With the other he worked a finger around her anus. Teasing it. Adding more bite to the pleasure.

"Yes, Alec. God, yes."

He pushed his finger past the tight ring of muscle and she bit her bottom lip. Like before, there was a burning sensation, but also one of white hot pleasure.

Jaya felt so full from his cock hitting her G-spot. Behind her, she could hear his moans. She could feel the way he gripped her hips as if he was afraid to let her go.

He loosened his grip on her hips and moved her to more of a standing position so he could kiss her neck. When he withdrew his cock, she cried out at the loss, begging for more.

"Hush, it's okay. I'm not leaving you. I'm just changing the angle." Gently laying her back on the table, he angled her hips lower and she felt the tip of his cock at the entrance of her pussy. The new angle had her moaning immediately. He felt so much bigger this way.

"Oh, God. Alec."

She tensed, and he immediately tried to withdraw. "No, Alec, just give me a second."

They stayed that way for what seemed like a lifetime, with only the head of his cock penetrating her. One hand on her breast, the other stroking her clit. The need rolled through her like a tidal wave and she breathed through the initial pain. She could feel the drops of sweat coming off him.

She moved against him and he pressed in farther, still playing with her nipple and stroking her slit. He withdrew until he was almost out and the pain was joined by the most intense pleasure.

"Alec."

His harsh whisper rang in her ears. "Is it starting to feel good?"

"Please, don't stop."

And he didn't. His strokes were measured, gentle. He took his time, even though clearly, he was holding back. She didn't want measured. She wanted raw, and fast. She wanted him to lose control.

Reaching between her legs, her fingers found his on her clit and they stroked together. The way he cursed in her ear was her only warning. He picked up the pace by a half measure and she felt every scorching ridge of him as he entered and retracted, aided by her juices. The hand teasing her nipple ceased to be gentle. As they both stroked her wet slit, she felt more of her juices on their joined fingers.

Another orgasm coiled inside her, this one threatening to tear her apart from the inside out. "Alec, please," was the only plea she was able to muster. She knew what she needed from him. Knew what she'd been craving. The complete and utter release of all her inhibitions.

As energy traveled from her toes to her fingertips and back, she could feel the walls of her pussy clenching around him.

She felt him trembling behind her as her body gripped him. "Jai!"

Heat and pleasure swamped her body as the orgasm rolled through her. Unable to wait for him, she drove her hips back, taking all of him that she could, her whole body shaking in ecstasy.

He wasn't far behind as his hands tightened on her hips and he drove into her once more, twice more. "Jesus, Christ." He bore down on her with his weight as his whole body quaked. As he came, he covered her body with his, holding her against him, making them one.

ALEC COULDN'T TAKE his eyes off of Jaya as she lounged on the settee, wearing nothing but his robe. He'd been so exhausted, he was partly inclined to stay in that booth forever, their bodies still joined. But he wanted to take care of her, so he'd carried her naked to the elevator. Through their ride up and their shower, he'd worked very hard to behave himself. He was so worried he'd hurt her. But there she was, wrapped in this robe looking fine. Better than fine.

"So, can I ask you a question?" Jaya chewed on her bottom lip in that habit of hers that drove him nuts.

"Knock yourself out." He tossed his towel in the hamper and crossed his arms in preparation.

"I know it's none of my business. I'm just that chick who—well, you know."

"Now you have me curious. What is it?"

"I've watched you."

He put on his usual bravado and swagger. "I've been watching you too."

She frowned. The tiny creases marring that smooth forehead. "Why do you do that? The moment I ask you to be serious, you start to play around. You're smart. Scary smart. Certainly smart enough to run a business. People like you, you've got charisma and charm. You could be running your own place or something. Instead, you're running around playing Guy Friday and Personal Assistant. It just doesn't jive."

The war that went on inside him was a quick one. Not sure what to reveal, he sighed. "When my mom died, I tracked my dad down. Before that, we'd never been in one location longer than six months or so. When I used to ask her about my father, she couldn't tell me much about him. Just that he'd been the adventuresome type. When I met him, he was married and couldn't stay still if you'd paid him money. And there was nothing he liked as much as he liked money."

Alec shrugged. "I'm sort of like him, I guess. I don't like the idea of being pinned down. Every time I have to stay anywhere permanent, it makes me itch. I have a hard time working at any one place for too long. I've been working for the Westhorpe's in one capacity or another since I was sixteen. Usually, I can work and nobody asks me questions or expects me to stay." At least that much was the truth. He was leaving in a day or so. What would be the point in telling her everything?

"But why not get a job or something you can travel with or put down roots? Aren't you a little worried about your future? I've got ulcers just thinking about how the heck you'll pay for retirement."

He shook his head. Of course she would worry about his retirement. The little voice in his head begged, screamed for him to take her seriously. She cared about him and what happened to him.

"Honestly, I'm fine."

"You might be fine, and good at your job. I just think you could be better."

And here it came, the proverbial shoe drop. "So I can't be just a bartender."

She slid off the settee. "I don't give a shit what you do if you're a bartender or CEO as long as you have fun and do what you want to do. You just seem like you're supposed to be doing so much more than taking orders from Adele. Like for you, this is the easier route to where you're going. If you're challenged, then great. But I doubt you can tell me you're challenging yourself."

"It's honest work."

"Of course it is. Honest work you can do. But I've talked to you. I know you're not being challenged, making sure Bambi and Trina show up on time for their shift. I see you frustrated with every part of this job. I see you frustrated having to take every call from Adele."

The lady had a point. But he couldn't concede that easily. She'd have his head when she found out he lied to her. "So you're telling me you wish I were more?"

She frowned. "What I'm telling you is that when I'm with someone I want that person to be happy. I want him to push to be the best version of himself. I aim for that every day. Some days I succeed at it. If someone were 'just'—" she used air quotes to emphasize her point. "—a personal assistant or whatever, if he was happy, I'd be happy. You're just going through the motions as if this is the next stop to somewhere else. You're marking time. Not just with me, but with Adele."

That last verbal dig lanced his side, sending white-hot pain of truth through the open wound. She'd hit the nail on the head without even knowing anything real or true about him. "Maybe I just haven't found anything important enough to make me challenge myself."

She moved toward him and planted a kiss on his lips. "Like I said, I'm just some girl you'll forget in two weeks. But I wonder if maybe you're not looking hard enough."

TWENTY-ONE

JAYA FIDDLED WITH THE STRAP OF HER DRESS. ALEC WOULD be here any moment to pick her up. They'd agreed to meet in the lobby, but he was late. She checked the understated silver Timex on her wrist. He was exactly three minutes later than the last time she checked. She'd worn this wholly inappropriate dress. The one-shoulder vermillion red number smoothed over her hips and curves. It was beautiful and she loved it. But red. Her father would have a fit. *But no one will be looking at your sister*.

The two halves of the argument cancelled each other out. Impatient, she sent Alec a text. *Where are you?* Before she could check her watch again, she saw him stride through her lobby in a tailored three-piece suit that looked like it had been made for him. She could only stare. He stopped as soon as he saw her. For several beats, neither of them moved an inch and Alec's mouth hung open.

Eventually, he moved woodenly toward her. His sandalwood scent enveloped her and she knew she was home. *Don't try and hold onto this one. He'll break your heart.*

Alec leaned in to give her a brief hug and she wanted to do nothing more than stay there. "Jaya, you look beautiful."

She smiled up at him. "You know how to flatter a girl."

He didn't return the smile. "I swear to God, if you ever go back to wearing grey, I'll tan your hide."

She raised an eyebrow at him. "My hide's already tanned."

The sexy smile of his flashed over his lips. "You're magnificent, do you know that?"

She ducked her head and whispered a thank you. "We need to go if we're going to make it up to La Costa in time."

He escorted her out of her building, hand placed lightly at the small of her back and she pretended for just the briefest of moments that this was real. That he was a real date and he loved her.

"I've got the perfect ride for the trip."

Jaya paused when she saw the Rolls Royce, complete with driver. "Oh Alec, are you serious?"

His smile was tight and she scrutinized him, trying to figure out the nuanced layers of what was wrong with this picture.

Alec's jaw ticked. "Jaya, I'm sorry."

Something unpleasant rolled in her belly. Something icy, and rotten and slimy. He did not have a *good news face* on. "What's wrong?"

He brushed a hair off her cheek. "Look, I'm really sorry to do this to you. I couldn't leave without telling you to your face, but I have to go. Tonight."

The hollow wound of another shoe dropping pounded in her head. "What do you mean you have to go? Where are you going?"

"I can't really explain right now. But I didn't want to just not show up. I'm on my way to the airport now. I didn't want you waiting around for me." He indicated the car. "I wanted to do something to make up for it."

No, this wasn't happening. She'd gotten dressed. She could see her father's face when she walked in without Alec. She needed him. He was leaving her. Rage coursed through her veins. Her voice chilled to frigid temperatures. "What the hell is so important you'd break our deal? An emergency expedition to Africa? Or maybe this mysterious project you've been working on? Or an emergency bartending project?"

The last one was a low blow. He didn't deserve that. She knew it. But she didn't care. She'd known what to expect from him, but she hadn't paid attention. This was her fault. Not his. Hers alone. She'd failed again. How the hell was she supposed to walk into that wedding now? She may play brave well, but at the core of it, she was a coward.

"Jaya, you have to know I'm sorry. But you know, you don't even need me."

"Can you hear yourself? If you were me, would you believe what you're saying?" something struck her. "Does this mean the gala job goes away as well?"

He frowned. "What? No. Adele hired you. I have nothing to do with it. Just because I have to leave right now doesn't mean I don't care about you. I wish it didn't have to be this way. You—"

"You know, I find it interesting that the moment you have to make the barest of commitments to something, you up and bail." She folded her arms. "You've never stuck to anything in your life. I was naive enough to think you'd stick with me."

"I know you're upset, but there is literally nothing I can do. It really is a matter of life and death."

She shook her head. "You're right. I don't need you. But this was a big deal to me. Maybe you're so used to bailing that you can't see that. You know what? Just go. Go on your mysterious adventure. I'll handle tonight by myself. Just like always."

TWENTY-TWO

ALEC BRACED HIMSELF AS THE CAR TOOK HIM FROM THE airport to the Menlo Park area in San Francisco. *Like it or not little brother, I'm coming to take you home.* The car pulled up to the townhouse with Alec having no clue what the hell he was going to say to his brother. Lucky for him, when he knocked, Max opened the door without even checking to see who it was.

"I've been expecting you. Adele is very determined." He swung the door open and staggered back into the living room area.

Alec entered into the dim hallway of the townhouse and closed the door behind him. A quick whiff and glance of the place told him all he needed to know. Max had been on a serious binge. The whole townhouse reeked of alcohol. It emanated from his brother's body. Stepping over a discarded T-shirt, he swore. "Shit, Max, you smell like a bar."

His brother plopped onto the couch. "Yep, and I look like shit, right?" He took a swig of some amber liquid. "I feel like it too."

Alec braced himself in the doorframe of the living room. "Get your shit. We're going back."

Max chuckled. "The fuck I am. You think you're the only one who can run away from your responsibilities?"

Ouch. Alec erected a mental wall to keep himself from seeing the image of Jaya standing there in her red dress as he told her he wouldn't be her date. "Nope. But my responsibilities don't include a wife-to-be and a kid. I didn't sign on for all that. But you, you're an ass."

Max made an attempt to get out of his seat, but flopped back down, blond hair falling away from his face. "So what you're saying is you were an ass when you left Sue five years ago?"

Alec breathed out a sigh. "Yeah. At least a little bit. But I wasn't engaged to her. She wasn't carrying my kid." He crossed his arms over his chest, hoping the action would keep him from wanting to pummel his brother. "To make matters worse, you've left her and the kid with a pile of shit to deal with. Drugs, Max. Seriously, did you think no one would find out?"

"It wasn't supposed to go like that. It was supposed to be a one-time deal. But after a couple of transactions, they wouldn't back off. I was just supposed to launder a fixed amount. Then they started to think I worked for them."

"The Sandovals have been looking for you. It's only a matter of time before they find you. You put Adele in danger, Sue, the hotels. Most importantly, your kid."

Max blanched. With a shaky hand he took another swig, and when his hand didn't stop shaking, he chugged again. "Yeah, well, my point exactly. That kid is better off without me. I can promise you that."

His brother's lackadaisical attitude set Alec's blood to simmer. "Oh yeah, had a conversation with the little one already, have you? God, you're such a self-important fuck-up. You have no concern for their safety? What if Sandoval and his thugs get a hold of Sue or the baby? You think they're going to play nice and wait for you to deliver what they think you took? They already paid Adele a visit. What that kid needs is his father to stand up and be a man."

"What do you know about it?" Max took the last sip out of the bottle and let it clatter to the ground.

"You're such a spoiled little shit. The spitting image and soul of the old man. You can't just run around doing what you want in life. You have to accept responsibility. You need to go back and deal with the Sandovals. Face Adele. She's been covering for you, but time's up. You really screwed up here." He shoved a hand in his hair.

Max pushed himself up off the couch, weaved, and then staggered to confront Alec toe to toe. "Look, this isn't your melodrama, okay? I just need some time to think. I couldn't think with everyone in my face all the time. I'll talk to Sandoval, tell him I don't have the transaction list he thinks I took."

"You really think it will be that simple? If Sandoval doesn't get what he wants, he'll take it out on Sue. Or at least, that's what he threatened her with."

Max swayed as he squeezed his eyes shut tight. "What do you mean threatened? Is-is she okay? Th-the baby?" His hands scrubbed his face. "I thought I had more time," he slurred.

Alec shoved him back on the couch. "I can't believe I gave up on Jaya to come and fetch you." He shook his head. "You don't have to worry. I'm not going to be Adele's errand boy anymore."

"I need to fix this."

"Finally, we're on the same page. Problem is, you say you

didn't take what they're looking for. Caleb thinks it's one of his lieutenants making a play by taking that transaction file. But they've pinned it on you for sure and they don't forgive that kind of fuck up."

"I'll take Sue and we'll run."

"Now is not the time to dick around. If you run, they'll find you. Caleb pulled some strings at the FBI. You'll talk to the feds and figure it out from there. You and the family might have to lay low for a bit, but Caleb is working on a solution."

"I'm a moron for getting into bed with them. I don't know what the hell I was thinking. It was so easy at first. Money Adele didn't control, didn't have a hawk eye on. Then they started asking for bigger and bigger cuts. Next thing I knew, I owed them money rather than the other way around."

Alec worked his jaw. "It could be worse. You just need to get home and fix it."

Max screwed up his face then mumbled a curse under his breath. "The night I left, I took the money out of my trust. I put half in a numbered account that couldn't be traced back to me. I paid part of the money I owed the Sandovals and planned to use the rest to take Sue away."

He blew out a breath. "I detoured to the office to talk to Adele, but she was closed in with the board. I hadn't planned to leave without saying anything to her. Even I'm not that callous. When I went back to my place, it was being searched. I figured something had come back to bite me in the ass so I'd better get lost for a minute. I didn't call Sue or Mom because I figured it would blow back on them." He shook his head.

"So you ran."

"I did it for their own good. It seemed like a good idea at the time."

TWENTY-THREE

Be brave, Jaya. You can do anything. In the last two weeks she'd done everything from standing up to her father, to leaving an old job for an even more terrifying new job, to skinny dipping, to seducing a man and having sex in all kinds of places she never thought about before. It was more than she'd lived in the ten years since her mother's death. If she could face those things and the new gold in her bedroom, she could face a room full of family, friends, and clients.

The clients she'd never had a problem facing. But somehow knowing she was going to hijack Tamara's thank you and welcome-to-my-wedding speech made the butterflies in her stomach jump and wiggle. She wished for Alec. But he was a crutch. She knew it. He was the force that propelled her, but she didn't need him.

He'd already changed her more in two weeks than anything else had. Love could do anything to someone. She inhaled a deep breath. Along the way to her table, she made stops, greeting those she knew. Her target in sight, she kept moving forward. All she needed was ten minutes with Brett James and she'd be done.

The loudspeaker went off and Tamara's jaunty lilt addressed the crowd.

Moving faster, Jaya worked through the crowd. If she could just get him aside for five minutes.

"Ladies and gentlemen. Thank you for joining us on this special occasion. Over the course of the week, we've played a little and laughed a little, and now on the day I take the next phase of my journey in life, I wanted to recognize the people who have helped me get here."

Jaya slipped into the seat next to James. "Hello, Mr. James. Nice to see you again."

He turned to face her, surprised. "Oh, yes. Jaya isn't it?" His gaze flitted back to Tamara and to her again. "The resemblance really is uncanny, you know."

She gave him a beatific smile. "Yes, we've been told that from time to time."

He chuckled. "What can I do for you?"

"You know, you're a hard man to get a hold of. I must have called your secretary a dozen times."

"I had no idea you were trying to reach me. Carol, my secretary, is a bit of a battleax. When I'm on vacation, she insists I'm on vacation. She won't put anything through unless it's life or death and sometimes, not even then."

"Well I wanted to speak to you about your upcoming project for the All-Tech conference. I want to make sure there are some aspects of the service you're aware of."

"Sure. I have to tell you, that Battlestar reference sealed the deal for us." He grinned. "But can we discuss in the morning? I already told your father that I want you heading the team. Your pitch was the most innovative and tailored. Everyone else pitched us like we were a bunch of marketing geared folks. They don't understand the Tech Geek set. They think we care about leggy models and bright colors. Models are nice, but I'm more interested in the next piece of tech."

Now was her chance. "Mr. James—"

"Brett, please."

First name basis, okay. "Brett, I'm sure my father is going to mention this in the morning, but I feel I have to tell you that I'm no longer with Trudeaux Events. Derrick Cooley will be in charge of your event."

He frowned. "You mean the one who attempted to distract me with pretty colors and not much substance?"

"I'm unaware of what he may have presented to you." Look at her, learning to be politically correct. "But he's got a unique skill. I'm sure—"

Brett's frown didn't lighten up. "I'll be discussing this with your father in the morning. Can I ask, what events company did you move to?"

Her brain blanked. Of all the plans not to have come up with. "JT Events. I'm an independent consultant. One of my first events will be the Westhorpe gala at the end of the year." Holy cow, had she just said that? Had she created her own company on the spot?

The frown lines on Brett's forehead disappeared. "The Westhorpe gala? That's no easy feat. Adele Westhorpe is known to be a—handful."

"She's not so bad." Maybe she was, but no one would hear that come out of Jaya's mouth.

"Tell you what. How about I give you a call after I speak with your father tomorrow?"

Jaya felt her head jerking up and down, but the synapses in her brain didn't fire enough to recognize actual words. But she got the gist. She had the All-Tech account if she wanted it. Holy shit.

"I suppose we can talk in the morning. Make sure to enjoy the champagne." Now, time to get out before she did any damage.

He raised his glass. "Don't you worry about that. I'm on my fourth glass." He looked around. "Where is your date? I assumed you'd be here with the Westhorpe guy? That was him with you at the rehearsal dinner, right?"

Her breath caught and she frowned. "Westhorpe?" A nervous giggle escaped her lips. That bad feeling that had been following her around like a lost puppy squeezed tight around her. "No. His name is Alec Danthers."

"That's a good point," he conceded. "But whether he likes it or not, he's Royce Westhorpe's oldest son. I met him in passing with his mother a couple of years ago. I didn't get the chance to talk to him at the rehearsal. I was hoping to catch up with him tonight."

Jaya's heart hammered. The rush in her ears drowned out all other sound. Excusing herself, she forced her body erect. She cleared her throat hoping she didn't look as befuddled as she felt. *Westhorpe?* "He was unavailable tonight."

"Always a shame to leave a beautiful woman unattended. Please make sure to save me a dance."

She gave him a wooden smile and excused herself, desperate for escape. As Jaya made her way back to her table, her legs trembled. Just like that, it had been as easy as a conversation. Brett James wanted her to manage their conference. And in the same breath, he'd told her the man she thought she'd been in love with wasn't who she thought.

She tried to process what that meant. *He's a Westhorpe?* She had a contract with Adele Westhorpe. Would the matriarch go back on the deal? Not likely. She may have given Jaya the job because of Alec, but Jaya was good and she knew it. And after everything, she didn't want to go back to Trudeaux. She could do this all on her own. At the same time, the All-Tech was the epitome of everything she'd ever wanted to do.

Too busy mulling over her choices, her brain didn't register Alec's lean frame in the doorway of the reception hall until she'd already walked past him. As dawning hit, she stopped, teetering on her heels ever so slightly. Her breath locked in her lungs and she couldn't breathe.

His voice was low. "I hope I'm not too late."

"I don't know what you're doing here, but I don't need you." Jaya brushed at the skirt of her dress as she stalked past him. She'd made it through this much of the wedding without him, so why did she feel a pang at the mere sight of him?

He nodded. "Okay, I deserve that. But hear me out." He took a step toward her.

The pull of his magnetism made her struggle for a minute, but she managed a step back. She'd already spent too much time trusting and believing in him. "I'm not sure exactly what I'm supposed to hear out. You mean about the part where you abandoned me when I needed you? Or about the part where you're a fucking Westhorpe?" She sniffed.

His shoulders stiffened and his lips thinned. "I'm not a Westhorpe. I'm nothing like my old man. Besides, he didn't want me, so it's not like I have a birthright to claim."

"Semantics, Alec. Adele Westhorpe is your step-mother.

You may not consider yourself a Westhorpe, but you have all the trappings. God. I've been so stupid."

"No, wait." He put up his hands. "Shit, it wasn't supposed to be like this. I wasn't supposed to be here more than two days. You assumed I was a bartender, and for that night I was. I just didn't tell you I was also the son of Royce Westhorpe. I never tell anyone. I'm ashamed of him."

She shook her head, unwilling to let him get out of it that easily. "You didn't need to lie to me, Alec. I wasn't after your money. You must have chuckled about poor Jaya. 'She doesn't even know I own the damn hotel.'"

"Come on, it wasn't like that. The penthouse suite *is* Max's. I want to be as far away from the Westhorpes as possible. I'm nothing like them. I spend more time exploring the world than following corporate greed."

"Oh, of course. Your adrenaline rushes." She dropped her head into her hands. "I'm such an idiot."

"Jaya, I came after you because you're the only one who made me feel something. I'd been chasing a rush for so long, I didn't know I could feel that rush with anyone."

"'Oh, and to ante up the adrenaline, let me lie to her and string her along.' I don't even know what to say. Did you fix your emergency, at least? Your matter of life and death?"

"I was able to find my brother. Caleb's arranged a deal for him with his contacts at the FBI. I think he'll be okay."

"So just like that, everything is okay?"

He frowned, his beautiful face taking on harsh lines. "No, not quite, but it's on its way."

She sighed. "Well, at least it was worth it."

"I'm sorry, Jaya. My dad, he was like Max." Softer, he added, "Like me, I guess. He couldn't stick around long. He left my mother when she was pregnant with me. I never knew who he was until my mom died and I found her documents. I went to find him so I could avoid the system. He didn't exactly want me around, but Adele took me in. Treated me like her own. Even after they had Max. She forced the old man to be a father."

"I'm sorry you had it rough, but it doesn't make up for your actions, Alec. I never want to see you again. I'm done." As she walked away, her eyes were dry. No use wasting any tears on him. The man she loved didn't exist.

TWENTY-FOUR

ALEC DIDN'T ANTICIPATE THE BURNING IN HIS LUNGS OR the pain that stabbed its way into his gut and hung around like a festering cloud. Was this what loving someone felt like? If so, it blew the big one. He watched her walk out and her father take steps to follow her.

Catching up with Pierre, he put a hand on his arm. "I don't think she'll want to be seeing either one of us right now."

If glares had temperatures, he had a feeling glacial would be how the man felt at the moment.

Pierre's look was hard and flat. "You're going to tell me how to handle my daughter? You've been lying to her all along, *Westhorpe*. You think I didn't know. I knew your father."

Alec nodded. The truth was a bitch. Especially when people kept grabbing it by the tail and bitch-slapping you with it. "Yes, I lied to her. For my own reasons. But at the end of the day I love her and I've lost my chance. If you love her, you can't keep treating her the way you do."

Pierre's hazel eyes narrowed. "And what do you know about

it? You're nothing but the bastard son with a trust fund and a hotel. You don't know my daughter."

"I know how she sounds when she laughs. I know what makes her cry, and I know she thinks you don't love her and that you favor her sister. I know she thinks you'd rather take the word of your son-in-law than hers." He drew in a breath. "I know if you don't take some steps to fix things with her, she'll be gone to you forever." He left out the unspoken *like I am.* But Pierre's expression grew grave and solemn.

"How can she think I favor her sister?"

Alec's eyes rolled of their own volition. "You fired her. Then made it impossible for her to get another job. What kind of father does that? I thought my dad was a harsh bastard, but you take the cake."

Pierre's lips flattened. "As I told her, I've never stood in her way. I let Jaya go for a slew of reasons, the most important being I wanted her to strike out on her own. And less importantly, because she, and my self-important son-in-law, would have eventually killed each other. You don't know my daughter. She has to figure things out on her own. I offered to call around and see if I could help her get another job."

Alec shoved his hands in his pocket. "You mean after you already called and told everyone she was unemployable?"

"What would I have to gain by doing that? I don't want her to fail. I do love her."

Alec held his breath. Jaya had been so sure it was her father who'd made those calls, but maybe it was someone else entirely. "Maybe, sir. It's time you talked to her. And not just talked, but listened too." He shrugged. "Maybe I should have tried that." Before turning to leave, he added, "And sir, you might also want to think about who else had something to gain by slandering Jaya around town."

TWENTY-FIVE

"Okay, so he left you," Micha said, brows drawn.

Ricca chimed in. "Then he came back to you, and still made it to the wedding reception."

Jaya nodded. "But it was a lie. All of it a lie. Who he was, his real name. Everything about him." The pain of it all still percolated in her belly, as if she'd swallowed an ample helping of boiling pain-and-regret soup. God, she felt sick. Sure, Alec had been clear about the whole relationship thing and she'd seen him as some fun to be had for a couple of weeks. She wasn't supposed to fall in love. So maybe that had been her fault. Love was a tricky animal. But he'd still abandoned her and lied.

The lies were the part she just couldn't swallow. She shook her head. "I must be a giant lie magnet." She circled her forehead with her index finger. "Big ol' target here that says, 'Yes, I'm easily duped and tread upon. Have at it. Do it for sport even.'" Feeling another pinprick behind her lids signaling yet another round of the *sniffle-sniffle* and *dab-dab*, she sniffed deeply and blinked hard to try and ward them off.

"You're not a fool, Jai. These things happen sometimes," Ricca tried.

Micha gave a quick shake of her head. "None of this is your fault. How the hell were you supposed to know he was a Westhorpe?" She shrugged. "So this whole time, Adele Westhorpe was his mother."

"Step-mother," Jaya corrected. "So now, I have to think about what all this means. Do I still have a job? Was she in on the whole thing?"

Ricca flopped back on Micha's duvet cover. "What are you going to do? Talk to her?" Jaya's head did the side-to-side routine again. "No. She's huge on professionalism. So I'm going to go to work on Monday and do my job. Until somebody shows up with security to show my black ass the door. It's the only thing I can do. And did I mention that Brett James wants to hire me to do the All-Tech?"

"Holy shit!" Micha gaped at her. "Again with the burying the lead."

Jaya pinned Micha with a stare. "Can we get back to what's important? Plan is I'm just going to status-quo it. For all I know, Adele has no idea about the shenanigans. All she'll notice is that Alec isn't around as much." Then a thought struck her. What if Alec didn't go to Durban like he'd said? What if he stayed? Then what would she do?

Oh, come on Trudeaux. Like he'd stay. He said himself he was not that guy. Always needed to be on the move. He wouldn't stay for her, so she needed to stop expecting the big grand gesture.

Micha picked up one of her wigs and adjusted it on her head. The pretty ringlet curls bounced around her shoulders cheerily.

Jaya was in no mood to be cheery. "How the hell did my life go to shit in a matter of weeks?"

Ricca did the usual hug-and-back-rub routine. *Pat-pat, rub-rub.*

Micha pinned her with a stare. "Sure. It's been a shitty two weeks, I give you that. But you know what? You got a job out of it. Shit, you got two. Your sister is actually, really trying with you, and maybe you'll repair your relationship. Plus you had the best sex of your life and you've crossed off some of your Thirty list. All in all, you gained, right?" She smacked Jaya on the shoulder. "And keep in mind, it's a job you actually like, despite the tyrant-like nature of your evil boss. Not to mention, Derrick is about to get fired by Brett James."

Good old Micha. Keeping it in perspective.

TWENTY-SIX

THIS WAS IT. THE FINAL CULMINATION OF ALL JAYA'S work. And the end of everything she'd started with he-who-she-refused-to-name-lest-she-have-to-find-him-and-shoot-him-between-the-eyeballs. The location was gorgeous. She'd been right. The industrial feel had been just what Adele was looking for. Though the old bird hadn't said it was perfect. She'd only said passable. But Jaya knew what she'd meant.

Over the last six months, Jaya had gotten to know her better. She wasn't as tough as she looked. Well, maybe a little, but it seemed they understood each other. Adele had never mentioned Alec. And Jaya had never mentioned that she knew of their relationship. They'd kept it professional. But having a client like Adele Westhorpe really did make your name. She already had three clients in the queue. She really was happier on her own.

Jaya had used some photos taken by a photographer from Paris to decorate, as well as lights. All kinds of tea lights hung from the ceiling and down from the artwork. Not too shabby, if she did say so herself. With a rush of pride, she stood on the platform overlooking the main party. The gallery had several semi-private balconies that patrons could use to view some of the artwork from above. It was really beautiful. Even the guest of honor put on her best. Not that Adele wasn't always dressed to the nines. But tonight she'd taken special care. She looked feminine, pretty in her blush-colored dress. Monique Lullier. Jaya had seen it in a magazine. For once she looked younger than her actual years. Soft, somehow. Not that Jaya would dare bring up that fact.

Adele joined her on the balcony. "Miss Trudeaux, I must say this event has shown to be..."

Passable, Jaya thought. After all, that was Adele's favorite word.

But Adele surprised her, continuing with, "extraordinary. It's exactly the feeling I wanted. Outstanding job."

Jaya couldn't help it. Her mouth did a fly-trap routine as she stared at Adele.

"Don't look at me like that, dear. You make me seem like I'm never nice."

"I-I-I didn't say you weren't nice. You are." Jaya tried hard with the lie.

Adele shrugged and settled a beaming smile on her. "At least you tried." She brushed at her skirts. "I know I can be... what do the assistants call me?" She tapped her finger on her chin. "A dragon lady."

Even as Jaya tried to deny what they both knew was truth, Adele held up her hand. "I know. I'm deliberately difficult. I test the mettle of people. But I'm loyal and I love deeply."

Jaya looked around surreptitiously. What had she done to deserve this level of honesty?

"You proved yourself over the last six months. And you put

up with me, which means you have more patience than sense sometimes. Not to mention more than once you've stood up to me. It's a skill I admire in an employee."

Not knowing what else to say, Jaya nodded and muttered "Th-Thank you, Miss Westhorpe."

"And let's stop that Miss Westhorpe nonsense, call me Adele. Everyone else does behind my back." She looked around at her guests. "I'd like you to stay on to do events for the hotel. All the top bill clients. If you're willing to think about it, we can discuss it in my office on Monday."

Holy shit. This was the kind of job she'd dreamed about. Except she didn't necessarily want that anymore. "Miss—" she changed course, "—Adele. Thank you for considering me for a job but—"

Adele smiled. "You want to run your own place?"

Jaya frowned. How had she—

"He said as much. So I'd like to retain your services on a contract basis. Would something like that work for you?"

Jaya's stomach knotted. *He. He. He.* Damn it. He-who-shall-not-be-named-lest-she-have-to-find-him-and-shoot-him-between-the-eyeballs was not behind this job offer. Could. Not. Be. Why did all her dreams come true feature him. Damn it. "Adele, thank you. Honestly, but—"

She laid a hand on Jaya's arm. "Think about it. I know you and my son aren't exactly on speaking terms, but maybe it's time you were. Besides, I would have hired you without his prompting. Don't let a man come between you and something you want. You'll always regret it." She turned and sauntered away to greet more guests.

Jaya watched after the woman a little surprised at their

exchange. Until now, she'd never gotten the impression Adele particularly liked her. Maybe that was just her way.

"You did an outstanding job, sweetheart."

Jaya whirled around to face her father. "I see you received your invitation."

"I was a little surprised to see it."

"Adele insisted."

Pierre shifted to his heels. "I must say I was also surprised you turned down the offer to come back to Trudeaux. I thought it was what you wanted."

Jaya nodded. "It was, but more about me not wanting to be a failure in your eyes than about me actually wanting to be at Trudeaux. I just wanted to be home."

Her father rubbed his nose. "Jaya, I'm sorry if you ever felt you weren't welcome at home. You were always so self-sufficient and such an individual, I knew Derrick would crush your spirit if you stayed."

"You chose your son-in-law over me, Dad."

"I know it doesn't make up for anything, but as soon as I found out it was Derrick who blocked you from any interviews, I fired him. It's not much. But I hope it can be a start."

Jaya didn't have any words for him. Of all the conversations she thought she'd be having, this wasn't one of them. "Dad, I don't even know where to start."

"How about over coffee. Monday?"

A real olive branch. From her father of all people. "I think I can manage that."

TWENTY-SEVEN

Alec watched Jaya with Adele. The woman of his dreams. The woman who had literally haunted him for six months. And here she was, right in front of him. So close he could reach out and touch. So why were his feet making like Crazy Glue with the floor?

For six months he'd tried to get the bitter taste of the last time he'd seen her out of his mouth, but cases of Lagavulin Scotch later, he still couldn't forget her. He hadn't left the way he'd wanted to. He hadn't said goodbye the way he'd planned to. Not that it mattered to her much. She'd done okay for herself. More than okay. He pumped Adele for information about Jaya and God bless the old woman, she'd scolded him then told him everything he'd wanted to know. She might be no nonsense, but she'd been a romantic once upon a zillion years ago.

Things were different now. He had something to offer Jaya. Something more than adrenaline chasing—on to the next job instability. He'd done the one stable thing in his life. Taken a job with Westhorpe, Inc. The new mantle of VP Operations felt a tad snug, but Adele had promised him wiggle room in the neck.

After all, Max had opted out. Hadn't he? Sure, Max was marrying Sue. Turned out, he was the marrying kind after all. And preparing to testify against the Sandovals.

He and Mimi had some issues to work on, but they were working through it. It wasn't even Adele who had suggested the gig to him. He went to her, crazy in the head from the mind-fuck of being away from Jaya. He'd asked if he could come home. Her answer—he'd never been the prodigal he thought himself.

So here he was. Maybe he could put himself out of his misery and talk to Jaya, or he could surprise the hell out of her when she got to the office on Monday and he was her new boss —or point of contact if she did what he thought she'd do and became a contractor.

They'd see each other all the time. The way he figured it; he could lay out his heart again. Well, fully this time. Tell her he loved her. That he couldn't live without her—he'd tried. And when it hadn't worked, he'd tried drinking the memory of her from his brain. And still remembered everything in the morning.

Stinger would be if she told him to pack it in. He'd told himself he could do it, but was that the truth? Could he just walk away from her and let her lead her life?

He navigated the throngs on a slow approach. He couldn't decide if a strong direct approach worked well or if he should try for surprise. *No surprises, asshole. Keep it direct.* He watched as both Adele and Pierre Trudeaux left Jaya standing alone, then took the stairs two at a time to the balcony she stood on, wiping his sweat slicked palms against his slacks.

You weren't supposed to do that to silk, but at this point, heart hammering in his chest, what did he care? There she was, in a teal, sexy, backless number, heels stacked so high she looked like she was teetering. They weren't the gold number she'd favored. This pair was black and metallic, but no less sexy than the pair she'd worn that first night she'd wrapped her legs around his hips. *Cool it. Focus*. He cleared his throat. Twice.

"Hi, Jaya."

She didn't even turn to face him.

He tried again. "Jaya."

She turned, pure disbelief etched tiny lines along her usually smiling mouth. The disbelief gave way to something that looked like worry, then something that looked like cold anger. And finally resolve.

"Alec. I didn't know you would be here." She smoothed an imaginary strand of hair off her face. "But of course I should have assumed. Is your brother in attendance? It would be great to get a family photo."

She still had a way with zingers. "Max won't be coming tonight. He's laying low while the Feds sort through his information on the Sandovals. It could be some time before he's home again." He shoved his hands in his pockets to keep them from pulling her into his arms. "In the meantime, I'll be taking over most of his duties at the Westhorpe as the new VP of Operations."

Her eyes widened and her lips parted. "So you're back for good." The wobble in her voice gave him hope.

"Yes, I am."

"That must be—difficult. I know you can't stand being in one place for too long."

"I—" Shit, why had he suddenly forgotten everything he was going to say? He tried again. Mouth open. No words. While his mouth did the guppy routine, he drank in every inch of her.

She looked beautiful. Right now he'd kill to have her make a list of tasks for him. Anything. "I've missed you."

Her response—*blink blink blink.*

Okay. So, not a good start. Once more with feeling. "You were right. I was a total prick. I was selfish and a liar. I never lied to you about how I felt, but I hid who I was from you. Deliberately. I didn't give you a chance to love me as I was. Instead, I gave you who I wanted to be. And that wasn't fair. I should have told you right from the start and there's no going back, but I'm sorrier than you know."

Now she pulled a guppy routine, so he kept going. After all, if you were going to cut open your chest, you might as well perform open heart surgery right? "I was a complete asshole for abandoning you. I knew you needed me, but I was in love with you and scared shitless, so I ran. I told myself I had a good reason. But it could have waited. I seized the excuse I had and ran with it. Then I wanted to apologize to you 'til the cows came home, but my secret slipped before I could explain everything."

"You left me." Her voice wobbled just a little.

He hung his head. "I should have tried harder. You were right. I was running. My whole life I've been running away. I can't keep running from you. I love you. And I know I don't deserve you. But if you would even give me the chance to—shit, I don't know, even be your friend, I'd take it." Except he knew he couldn't be her friend. Shit, were those tears pricking at his eyes? Damn it. He was a full on pussy. "I've really missed you."

Her chin went up, but there was a shimmer in her eyes. "What happens when things get hard and I ask you to commit to something? Are you going to bail again?"

"No. I swear to you. I belong here with you. I tried to leave you behind and forget you, but there was no getting you out of my head. I'm not going to say I don't like adventure, I do, but we can go on them together. Without you, none of it held any meaning or value for me."

She shifted in her shoes. "Give me one good reason why I should trust you. Why I should believe that you're here for good and won't just get on a plane tomorrow?"

Here it was. His hands started to shake. It seemed like the whole room slowed down to the speed of a sloth. Shoving a hand in his pocket, he slowly bent to one knee and grabbed the small velvet box inside. Opening it, he cleared his throat. "Because I'm willing to give you the stars."

Her mouth fell open as she gaped at the ring. Had he gotten it wrong? Gone too big? Too small? Maybe the star was too childish. Shit. This was all sorts of wrong.

He dared a peek into her eyes and they were brimming over with tears. From the distance he heard someone shout, "For the love of God, Jai, put the man out of his misery already. You've been pining for months. Everything you want is right in front of you. You going to throw it away?" He would remember to give Micha a giant hug later. Well maybe buy her a drink and forego the hug.

Jaya stared at the ring. Then stared back at him. She slowly walked over to him and pulled him to his feet. The crushing despair. He thought he could die of it. A soft hand went to his face.

"I would take you without the ring."

"I know. That's precisely why I want you to have it. You're gorgeous and smart and could organize an ant colony to make it more efficient. And your lists. I've missed your endless lists and your attempts to manage my chaotic life. I want it all with you. Be my wife."

The kiss she gave him was soft, but determined. Hope bloomed in his chest. "Yes, Alec. I'll marry you."

"Well, it's about damn time," both Micha and Adele said as they stood shoulder to shoulder under the balcony. Adele sniffed and added, "I've always wanted a daughter."

Alec held her close, relief pouring from his soul. As he embraced Jaya, he whispered into her ear. "No more running away. I will never leave you." He sealed the promise with a kiss.

The End.

♛

THANK you so much for reading SEXY IN STILETTOS!

I hope you loved Alec and Jaya. Find out what's next for them. Order STROLLERS & STILETTOS & STILETTOS now so you don't miss it!

"LACHLAN KING CAUGHT **naked kite surfing with Hollywood Starlet!" "Scandal Rocks King Family... Again!" "King Media Family furious with out of Control Second Son!"**

Yeah, I've seen the headlines too.

My family is threatening to disown me if I get near another bloody scandal.

So I'm staying out of trouble. Or trying to...until I see her.

It doesn't matter that she's dancing with someone else. The moment our gazes meet across a crowded club, I know one thing. I have to have her. Even though, I can tell from just looking at her, she's going to get me in trouble.

One night is all I'll need.

Famous last words.

One-click THE HEIR now!

Can't get enough billionaires? Meet a cocky, billionaire prince that goes undercover in **Cheeky Royal**! He's a prince with a secret to protect. The last distraction he can afford is his gorgeous as sin new neighbor.

His secrets could get them killed, but still, he can't stay away...

Read Cheeky Royal now!

Turn the page for an excerpt from Cheeky Royal...

SNEAK PEAK OF CHEEKY ROYAL

"You make a really good model. I'm sure dozens of artists have volunteered to paint you before."
He shook his head. "Not that I can recall. Why? Are you offering?"

I grinned. "I usually do nudes." Why did I say that? It wasn't true. Because you're hoping he'll volunteer as tribute.

He shrugged then reached behind his back and pulled his shirt up, tugged it free, and tossed it aside. "How is this for nude?"

Fuck. Me. I stared for a moment, mouth open and looking like an idiot. Then, well, I snapped a picture. Okay fine, I snapped several. "Uh, that's a start."

He ran a hand through his hair and tussled it, so I snapped several of that. These were romance-cover gold. Getting into it, he started posing for me, making silly faces. I got closer to him, snapping more close-ups of his face. That incredible face.

Then suddenly he went deadly serious again, the intensity in his eyes going harder somehow, sharper. Like a razor. "You look nervous. I thought you said you were used to nudes."

I swallowed around the lump in my throat. "Yeah, at school whenever we had a model, they were always nude. I got used to it."

He narrowed his gaze. "Are you sure about that?"
Shit. He could tell. "Yeah, I am. It's just a human form. Male. Female. No big deal."

His lopsided grin flashed, and my stomach flipped. Stupid traitorous body...and damn him for being so damn good looking. I tried to keep the lens centered on his face, but I had to get several of his abs, for you know...research.
But when his hand rubbed over his stomach and then slid to the button on his jeans, I gasped, "What are you doing?"
"Well, you said you were used doing nudes. Will that make you more comfortable as a photographer?"

I swallowed again, unable to answer, wanting to know what he was doing, how far he would go. And how far would I go?

The button popped, and I swallowed the sawdust in my mouth. I snapped a picture of his hands.

Well yeah, and his abs. So sue me. He popped another button, giving me a hint of the forbidden thing I couldn't have. I kept snapping away. We were locked in this odd, intimate game of chicken. I swung the lens up to capture his face. His gaze was slightly hooded. His lips parted...turned on. I stepped back a step to capture all of him. His jeans loose, his feet bare. Sitting on the stool, leaning back slightly and giving me the sex face, because that's what it was—God's honest truth—the sex face. And I was a total goner.

"You're not taking pictures, Len." His voice was barely above a whisper.

"Oh, sorry." I snapped several in succession. Full body shots, face shots, torso shots. There were several torso shots. I wanted to fully capture what was happening.
He unbuttoned another button, taunting me, tantalizing me. Then he reached into his jeans, and my gaze snapped to meet his. I wanted to say something. Intervene in some way...help maybe... ask him what he was doing. But I couldn't. We were locked in a game that I couldn't break free from. Now I wanted more. I wanted to know just how far he would go.

Would he go nude? Or would he stay in this half-undressed state, teasing me, tempting me to do the thing that I shouldn't do?

I snapped more photos, but this time I was close. I was looking down on him with the camera, angling so I could see his perfectly sculpted abs as they flexed. His hand was inside his jeans. From the bulge, I knew he was touching himself. And then I snapped my gaze up to his face.
Sebastian licked his lip, and I captured the moment that tongue met flesh.

Heat flooded my body, and I pressed my thighs together to abate

*the ache. At that point, I was just snapping photos, completely in
the zone, wanting to see what he might do next.*

"Len..."
*"Sebastian." My voice was so breathy I could barely get it past
my lips.*
"Do you want to come closer?"
"I--I think maybe I'm close enough?"
*His teeth grazed his bottom lip. "Are you sure about that? I have
another question for you."*

*I snapped several more images, ranging from face shots to shoul-
ders, to torso. Yeah, I also went back to the hand-around-his-dick
thing because...wow. "Yeah? Go ahead."*
"Why didn't you tell me about your boyfriend 'til now?"
*Oh shit. "I—I'm not sure. I didn't think it mattered. It sort of feels
like we're supposed to be friends." Lies all lies.*
He stood, his big body crowding me. "Yeah, friends..."
*I swallowed hard. I couldn't bloody think with him so close. His
scent assaulted me, sandalwood and something that was pure
Sebastian wrapped around me, making me weak. Making me
tingle as I inhaled his scent. Heat throbbed between my thighs,
even as my knees went weak. "Sebastian, wh—what are you
doing?"*
"
Proving to you that we're not friends. Will you let me?"
*He was asking my permission. I knew what I wanted to say. I
understood what was at stake. But then he raised his hand and
traced his knuckles over my cheek, and a whimper escaped.*

His voice went softer, so low when he spoke, his words were more like a rumble than anything intelligible. "Is that you telling me to stop?"

Seriously, there were supposed to be words. There were. But somehow I couldn't manage them, so like an idiot I shook my head.

His hand slid into my curls as he gently angled my head. When he leaned down, his lips a whisper from mine, he whispered, "This is all I've been thinking about."

Read Cheeky Royal now!

Royals United

Royal Tease
Teasing the Princess

Royal Elite

The Heiress Duet

Protecting the Heiress
Tempting the Heiress

The Prince Duet

Return of the Prince
To Love a Prince

The Bodyguard Duet

Billionaire to the Bodyguard
The Billionaire's Secret

London Royals

London Royal Duet

London Royal
London Soul

Playboy Royal Duet

Royal Playboy
Playboy's Heart

London Lords
See No Evil

Big Ben
The Benefactor
For Her Benefit

Hear No Evil
East End
East Bound
Fall of East

To Catch a Thief

Speak No Evil
London Bridge
Bridge of Lies
Broken Bridge

The Donovans Series
Come Home Again (Nate & Delilah)
Love Reality (Ryan & Mia)
Race For Love (Derek & Kisima)
Love in Plain Sight (Dylan and Serafina)
Eye of the Beholder – (Logan & Jezzie)
Love Struck (Zephyr & Malia)

London Billionaires Standalones
Mr. Trouble (Jarred & Kinsley)
Mr. Big (Zach & Emma)
Mr. Dirty (Nathan & Sophie)

The Shameless World

Shameless
Shameless
Shameful
Unashamed

Force
Enforce

Deep
Deeper

Before Sin
Sin
Sinful

Brazen
Still Brazen

The Player
Bryce
Dax
Echo
Fox
Ransom
Gage

The In Stilettos Series
Sexy in Stilettos (Alec & Jaya)
Sultry in Stilettos (Beckett & Ricca)
Sassy in Stilettos (Caleb & Micha)

Strollers & Stilettos (Alec & Jaya & Alexa)
Seductive in Stilettos (Shane & Tristia)
Stunning in Stilettos (Bryan & Kyra)

~~~

In Stilettos Spin off
Tempting in Stilettos (Serena & Tyson)
Teasing in Stilettos (Cara & Tate)
Tantalizing in Stilettos (Jaggar & Griffin)

Love Match Series
Game Set Match (Jason & Izzy)
Mismatch (Eli & Jessica)

Don't want to miss a single release? Click here!
~~~

ABOUT NANA MALONE

USA Today Bestselling Author, Nana Malone's love of all things romance and adventure started with a tattered romantic suspense she borrowed from her cousin on a sultry summer afternoon in Ghana at a precocious thirteen. She's been in love with kick butt heroines ever since.

Nana is the author of multiple series. And the books in her series have been on multiple Amazon Kindle and Barnes & Noble bestseller lists as well as the iTunes Breakout Books list and most notably the USA Today Bestseller list.

www.ingramcontent.com/pod-product-compliance
Lightning Source LLC
Chambersburg PA
CBHW010427120726
47992CB00010B/3355